POOL PARTY

Marilynn Tebbit

Pool Party
Copyright © 2022 by Marilynn Tebbit

This is a work of fiction, not a memoir! Of
course, I tried to capture the essence of
Tampa at the turn of this most recent century
and what might have been possible, but the
tale is pretty much a mountain conjured
from a pebble, or from nothing at all, save
for my overactive imagination. Enjoy!

Tellwell Talent
www.tellwell.ca

ISBN
978-0-2288-7470-6 (Paperback)
978-0-2288-7471-3 (eBook)

Dedication

To V.L. Murray and Nancy Bell, the editors of MuseItUp Press, who originally accepted *Pool Party* for e-publication in 2013.

Thank you to Nancy Lee for telling me about the Surrey International Writer's Conference, where the novel was picked up.

Also, for my creative writing professor at the University of Calgary, Aritha van Herk, who expended great amounts of energy trying to make us the best writers we could be. And Mr. Robin MacKay of Fenwick, Ontario, my Grade 13 English teacher who very much encouraged my writing.

1. Exit Calgary—
September, Early 2000's

"You're really doing this." Dennis stared at the square of paper Marcie had given him with her new Florida address on it.

"I told you I was."

"Yeah, but a lot of people say they're gonna do stuff and never do." His eyes drifted to her packed boxes, scattered around what wouldn't be Marcie's living room much longer.

"I'll still illustrate your next book. I'll email you the drawings, so let me know when you get email, then you can tell me what changes to make, and then I'll send you the hard copies."

Dennis nodded, then continued to brood. "I'm jealous. You can just leave."

"I'm not married with kids," Marcie taunted, the reason Dennis gave for not sleeping with her. Married men in the bar did. Then apologized after for their mistake—her. Stepping out on their wives. Cheating. That'd change in Florida. No more being a drunken mistake. In Florida, she'd start over fresh. Easier when she wouldn't be working in a bar.

Marcie tucked in a flap on a box of winter clothes slated for donation, while Dennis simmered with wish-lust for her. Staying in Calgary longer wouldn't change his mind about remaining a faithful husband and dad, so her time in what she called the sub-Arctic dirt bowl was done. Even if the five-minute fucks continued south of the border, at least she'd be warmer, thanks to *Dodger the Dog.* Her cut of the profits, plus her savings, should buy her a frugal year on the Gulf Coast, even if she couldn't sell anything else, although Dennis already had plans for their next book. Her rent for the first six months had been paid, the only way she could obtain an apartment.

He held out his arms for a goodbye hug, which, if he were any other man would have led to bed, but Dennis just held her. She wished she had the strength to overpower a man, but pinning him to the ground against his will wouldn't exactly work to make him hard.

"If we were to," Dennis justified his inaction, "you know, do anything, my belongings would end up like yours. Packed in a box. Maybe when I'm a super-famous children's author, Julia won't care what I do, and I could at least visit."

"You have my address."

"You never know. One day when it's fifty below . . ."

"I won't be holding my breath."

"Call to let me know that you got there, okay?" He kissed the top of her head.

"As soon as I get a phone," she promised, closing the door behind Dennis, then sang, "Oh, say can you see? By"—or was it *from*?—"the dawn's early light." The only words she recalled from America's national anthem after fourteen years of listening to it on big-screen TV prior to sporting events, often several times per shift.

"I'm just going down for six months," Marcie rehearsed in the customs line. Perfectly legitimate. And legal. She was a snowbird. She even had a return ticket—though an open-ended one—and to Vancouver—a place where the grass was at least green and the temperature range less psychotic. And to explain the art supplies? She'd need something to do on a long holiday. The photo albums and numerous copies of *Dodger the Dog* might be more difficult to pass off. Why would she need to drag along memories and so many copies of the same book on a vacation? But, no, she wouldn't have to explain either of those; they were in her suitcase, already loaded onto the plane. All she had with her right now were her purse and carry-on, containing one copy of *Dodger,* her bank book, charge card, and rent receipts: proof she wouldn't be bumming around or illegally seeking work. Selling paintings wouldn't be taking a job away from an American, so she shouldn't feel like she was trying to pull something off. Customs agents were likely trained to sniff guilt.

"Hi." Marcie gave the agent her most charming grin as she stepped up to the bulletproof Plexiglas and slipped her paperwork underneath.

The official gave it a glance. "You're the youngest snowbird to come through here in a while."

"I got lucky with a children's book." She held up *Dodger the Dog* and tapped her name after "Illustrated by."

"Congratulations. Enjoy the sun." He stamped her passport, dismissing her into her dream.

"Thank you." Marcie smiled, concentrating on keeping a poker face. An overhead camera reminded her to maintain her composure until she boarded the plane. Only then did she break into a grin, like she'd escaped prison.

2. Arrival in Tampa

Humidity and warmth seeped into the cabin as soon as the flight attendants opened the door upon landing in Tampa. After she'd collected her luggage and cleared customs, Marcie flagged a cab. Her gated community wasn't supposed to be far from the airport. As the driver sped down wide roads, she stared at the palm trees, downed power lines, felled metal light poles, boarded-up windows, roofs missing chunks of shingles, and a general array of debris scattered randomly along the roadside. Evidence of the recent hurricanes she'd seen on the news, but a little superficial damage seemed a small price to pay for no winter. Which was when hurricanes—known as blizzards—happened in Canada, though they never chewed up any roofs. Either Canadian homes were built tougher or the cold froze the shingles in place.

Garbage half-filled the ditches, and the road's shoulders glistened with broken glass. American flags flew from the tops of buildings and were staked into front lawns. When stopped at traffic lights, Marcie stared, fascinated by the hubcaps spinning backwards on the cars next to her. Intoxicating combinations of Latin and reggae music blasted from the vehicle windows, as brown drivers wearing backwards baseball caps bobbled their heads to the new-to-her beat.

Minutes later, her driver turned down a lane leading to a walled-in property and stopped in front of the rental office. Having no American cash, she paid and tipped by credit card, then helped the driver hoist her bags out of the trunk.

On the other side of the gate sprawled a paradise of palm trees, flowers, a duck pond, and a fenced-in swimming pool. Home! Enchanted, she turned the knob to the rental office before noticing the CLOSED sign.

Impossible. At three-thirty in the afternoon? She stared down at the dozens of lizards, darting in every direction. But, no, five-thirty, with the time change. She reset her watch. But management knew she was coming. They should have . . . what, waited? Just for her? She lifted the mat to see if anyone had left her a note or key to her suite. No.

So what now? She walked up to the pedestrian gate and looked through. The mosquitoes must be bad here; screens enclosed all the balconies. In Calgary, no one even had screens on their windows or doors.

She contemplated what to do next. Waste half a month's grocery money on a hotel or wait for someone to come home and follow them in through the gate? If she explained her situation, maybe they'd let her into the pool, where she could spend the night on a chaise. Not like she'd freeze here. And, with so many fences and electronic locks, she'd feel perfectly safe. Though, if she wanted, she could probably roll herself under the car gate. And if she could, couldn't anyone? Not if they didn't want to be caught on camera. Though, why should she care? She lived here. If someone called the police, she could show them her rental receipts.

She shoved her suitcase, her carry-on, and her purse under the gap, and rolled under the car gate to set off in search of her new home.

She quickly located it in the first outdoor hallway from the gate, on the ground floor, facing the parking lot. Not a great view, except of the tops of palm trees towering over the fence, but she wouldn't be spending a lot of time inside staring out the window. Maybe the office had left the door open for her. She tried the knob. Nope. Key under the mat? No to that, too. Disappointed, she lugged her bags toward the pool.

Empty. Unbelievable in such a perfect climate, though people were probably eating dinner right a. She tried opening the pool gate, but it was locked too. So, she'd wait. Someone should want a dip after dinner. Or to read the paper waterside, in the hot humid air. She found a rock to perch on and read more of her book until she needed to use a bathroom. The grocery store or either of the two fast-food places at the end of the lane should have one. Or the discount store, also nearby. She needed to grab a bite anyway. Not wanting to haul her luggage, she concealed it behind a bush, opened the pedestrian gate—possible from the inside—stuck a twig in to prevent the gate from closing, and headed for the closest burger joint.

The inside of the restaurant felt like a deep freeze, yet none of the customers seemed uncomfortably cold. Marcie crossed her arms to retain body heat while she ordered a salad and apple juice, then waddled off to the bathroom and returned to the deserted pool area with dinner.

Preferring to save her evening meal for when she could actually sit at a table, Marcie stashed it next to her suitcases and walked around to explore. Paved sidewalks surrounded by giant plants with huge leaves led to each block of apartment homes. Big, white birds with long orange beaks and legs prowled the leafy underbrush.

Marcie took her new digital camera out of her purse and snapped photographs, perfect to include in *Tim the Tomcat*. Give it a Florida touch. The larger purple birds wading in the duck pond would make great subject matter, as well.

When it suddenly got too dark to see, Marcie looked at her watch. Only seven o'clock! It was still warm. Weird. Hot and dark at the same time. Almost unheard of in Calgary, even in the middle of summer, except for a handful of evenings. She made her way back to the pool.

Finally, some people! A group of men sat playing cards. They'd even left the gate open. Marcie brought her suitcases in and claimed a table a respectful distance away. She watched for someone to look up and notice her so she could wave and say hi, but they were all very involved in their game. She opened her salad and juice.

"Hey! You can't do that!"

Marcie looked up.

"That's cheating!"

"Yeah? According to whose rules?" A man across the table, close enough to be heard at a lower volume, shouted back,

"That's standard."

"Show me where it says . . ."

All six bickered before continuing their game, reaching, leaning, drinking from plastic cups, hunching, stretching, making faces, clutching or throwing cards, and talking; all in all, behaving nothing like the static, stoic, poker players on TV. Marcie fiddled with the light settings on her camera, zoomed in on their explosive energy, and snapped several shots to paint from.

Finally, the short brown man threw down his hand and stood up, knocking over his chair. "You all cheat." He stormed off, bumping the table and probably knocking over everyone's chip piles, judging by the resulting chaos.

When order was restored, the tallest man waved to Marcie. "Come join us. Take his place. Please."

"I don't play cards," Marcie warned.

"Neither does he."

Marcie grabbed her drink, salad, and purse, and walked over to meet her new neighbours.

"Fancy." Tall Guy tapped her camera lens sticking out of her purse.

"I'm an artist. I use it for reference pictures," Marcie explained, noticing the gorgeous blond man staring at her as he would at a ghost or the most captivating thing he'd ever laid eyes on. She stared back with equal intensity.

"You're gonna draw us? See, I always knew I was a work of art," Tall Guy bragged.

"You're a piece of work," Blond God corrected.

"Says the pot."

"I'm puttin' my life together. Yours is still goin' downhill."

"Whose turn is it?" The shorter of two Black men reminded his cohorts of the game.

"You in that much of a hurry to lose the rest of those?" Blond God pointed at Short Black Guy's five chips while restacking his own tower.

"Just wait." Short Black Guy took a swig of his beer and slammed down the can. "This game ain't over."

"You do more drinkin' than playin'." Blond God took a swig from his bottle of water, then looked back at Marcie. "You just move in?"

"Yeah, but I missed office hours, so I can't get into my place."

"Stay with me," four of the five offered at once.

"I'd love to." She stared at Blond God, accepting his invitation.

"You need a drink." Tall Guy offered.

"I have one." Marcie pointed to her apple juice.

"That's not a drink. Here." Tall Guy unscrewed the cap from a glass bottle of vodka, even though a sign said, NO GLASS BY THE POOL, and poured.

"Whoa." Marcie pulled back her juice. "Not half-and-half."

"Welcome to Palm Grove." Blond God grinned.

"You Canadian?" Tall Guy guessed.

"How'd you know?"

"I can tell by your accent. I'm Pat. From New Hampshire." He reached out to shake hands and held on a long time. "That's Tim," he said, referring to Blond God, "starting his life over fresh after divorce and his tenth stab at detox, from New Jersey. A real catch. These two reprobates . . ."

"Please don't lump us together," the short and slightly more awake Black guy held up his hand.

"You live in the same place," Pat justified.

"Only 'cause I can't get him offa my couch."

"I'm off it now," the taller Black guy pointed out.

"As I was saying, these two are Jim,"—he pointed to the shorter one—"who has a job at the airport, and Abe, inertia personified, from *Detraat,* who doesn't work."

"I work, Mr. *Baastan.*" Abe exaggerated Pat's accent, without moving from his slouched position in his deck chair.

"I meant legal work. Driving for that piece-of-shit waste-of-flesh"—Pat stared in the direction the man who'd run off had gone—"isn't a job. And, last *and* least, half-passed out and pissed off 'cause he's losing again, meaning his rich-bitch, old-lady from Texas is gonna kill him, Okey-dokey Ken from Oklahoma City."

"*Fuck* you," Ken muttered.

"So," Pat summed up. "You're in good company. Nobody's from here. And if you want to stay, I'll marry you," he volunteered.

"Yeah, well you better get divorced first," Blond Tim pointed out. She couldn't let Dennis name the tomcat Tim now.

"At least I'm not still in love with my ex," Pat defended himself. "Tim might be divorced on paper, but he mopes like a teenager over the woman he cheated on so many times that she ran off with somebody else."

"Both those guys are used goods." Jim nodded toward Pat and Tim. "Me, I never been married."

"By thirty-five? Red flag." Abe the driver shook his head. "Which leaves me." He puffed out his chest. "I'm a fresh twenty-two."

"Fresh out of jail," Pat pointed out.

"An' I learned my lesson." Abe didn't deny having done time.

"Yeah. How not to get caught again. Don't make it sound like you turned over any new leaf. Okay, your turn now. Tell us about you." Pat turned to Marcie.

"I'm Marcie, from, as you guessed, Canada." She didn't want to have to explain Calgary, Alberta.

"You must do something important to be able to get a work visa to come here," Abe assumed.

"Technically, I'm a snowbird. I can't work. I'm an artist. I got lucky with a children's book, so I want to try to make my living here as an artist."

"So you're famous?" Jim concluded.

"No. Not with one book. You didn't say what you do." Marcie turned to Pat.

"I work Collections for a bank," Pat answered. "Tim's a mechanic. Ken's a gigolo, though not for much longer if he don't learn to play cards. Chrissy's goin' broke."

"For once, that little Hispanic shit's right. You guys do cheat," Ken condemned.

"I'm glad I ain't you, man." Jim shook his head at Ken.

"What are you gonna tell her this time?" This from Tim.

"*Fuck* off, all-a-you." Ken stomped off into the shadows.

"So." Jim grinned. "Do we get to look at your art?"

Marcie turned on her camera and scrolled through a few shots of pieces she'd auctioned off at her goodbye party. "I just got the camera, so that's all I have. Except this." She tugged *Dodger the Dog* out of her purse.

Jim tilted the book toward the lighted pool so he could see. "Management's too cheap to install decent lights." He flipped through the pages.

"I got lights," Pat pointed out.

"'Bout all," Tim scoffed. "He's still paying for the house his wife lives in up north."

"I got more than just lights." Pat slapped himself in the crotch. "Mine still works. All those pills you're taking, you're probably as soft as your bed."

Tim said nothing. Marcie shifted uncomfortably, wondering if what Pat said was true.

"You did these?" Jim broke the awkward silence, closing *Dodger* and handing it back.

"Yeah." A large winged insect pinged off Marcie's skin. "What was that?"

"Time to go in." Jim gathered up the cards and chips. "Who's in for dinner?"

"If you're buyin'. 'Cause I was winnin'," Tim pointed out.

"You comin'?" Pat invited. "And don't say you already ate. Salad's not food and you didn't even finish it."

"Sure," Marcie accepted. "What should I do with my suitcases?"

"You can keep 'em at my place," Tim offered first.

"You better ask if she's allergic to cats."

"You have a cat? The next book I'm illustrating has a cat in it. Maybe I could take some pictures."

Pat rolled his eyes.

"Sure." Tim shrugged, still grinning.

"Just make sure you don't let him get hold of your camera," Pat cautioned. "Or you'll have more pictures than you bargained for, and who knows where they'll end up. Tim has a computer."

"I ain't like that no more," Tim swore.

"Yeah, you could be right. All that medication you're on. Only thing that excites him now is TV."

Tim picked up one of Marcie's suitcases. "*Holy shit.* Whatcha got in here?"

"Photographs. Copies of *Dodger* I'm hoping to sell. Know anybody with kids?"

"I'll buy one. Someday I—"

"You want kids?" The bottom fell out of Marcie's stomach. She didn't. And wouldn't. Ever. Not even for Tim.

"Yeah. You?"

"No."

"Why not? They're cute. Those happy little voices. All their energy."

There went that hope. For the long term. But maybe for the meanwhile, until he found somebody to have his kids with, they could . . . "Are you seeing anybody right now?"

"No."

"Maybe we could . . . till you find . . ."

"I'm not ready to have no girlfriend yet. I've only been sober a year. My shrink says I can try, but, I just don't feel ready."

"Oh." Marcie hung her head sadly.

"Plus, you remind me of my ex-wife."

Which explained why he'd stared at her like that. Not because he was attracted to her. And now he didn't want history repeating itself. Maybe once he realized she wasn't like his ex and that things could be different . . . He just gave off a warm, powerful energy, drawing her to him, which, plus his visual appeal, made him intoxicating. Plus, they had something in common: they'd both quit their old lifestyles. Together, they could explore the new people they were growing into. She'd just have to make him see that.

Marcie followed him past her breezeway into the next one and up one flight of stairs to where he lived. A blast of cold air similar to that in the burger joint hit her when he opened his door. What was with these people and air conditioning? If they liked cold so much, why didn't they stay north? Seventy-four, she peeked at the thermostat. Warm enough anywhere else, but not coming in from ninety-five. Anticipating that the restaurant would also be cold, Marcie grabbed a sweater out of one suitcase before following Tim to the gate and joining the others.

"Abe pass out?" Tim noticed him missing.

"What else?" Jim confirmed.

Ken had already peeled off, which left Jim, Pat, Tim, and her.

Pat stopped in front of the first restaurant that didn't have a lineup. It reminded Marcie of a chain she detested in Calgary because of the way management treated its staff, who were hired only if the managers wanted to sleep with them. And when the girls got past age twenty-three? Goodbye, because older women didn't put up with shit, like coming in just to sit around, unpaid, waiting to go on shift until business warranted another server on the floor; doing unpaid clean-up at the end of a shift; blowing the boss in the back; paying for walk-outs and mistakes; tipping out the *house,* in addition to the hostess, bartender, bussers, bouncers, and kitchen, even if that meant paying out of pocket, because tip-outs were calculated on ring-outs and not a percentage of actual tips. Which meant going to work could cost money. Only those in management and their friends got the good shifts and the most hours. Anyone who didn't get enough to survive on quit in disgust, unless they were living at home and worked only for the fun, glamour, and free booze. They stayed until they were too wrecked to function, then were fired when they hadn't even been getting a pay cheque. *You drank it,* management would claim.

"Comin'?" Tim's voice brought Marcie back to the present.

"Can we sit on the patio?" *Away from the negative vibes coming from the toxic atmosphere inside.*

"You really aren't from here, are you?"

Marcie frowned, puzzled. "What's wrong with sitting outside? It's warm." But the patio was empty, so something had to be wrong with it.

"In a few more weeks, maybe, when it's too cold for 'em, but not yet."

"Too cold for what?"

"Come on." Tim took her hand, but she remained rooted. What would she do if she couldn't support herself as an artist in Florida? She couldn't go back to waitressing in Canada if she couldn't even walk into a restaurant. Even the word gave her the heebie-jeebies. *Waitress.* Lower than dirt. Bar slut. Nobody any so-called respectable man wanted to be publicly seen with. At least in BC, where she'd be going instead of returning to Alberta, the minimum wage was higher, so she might be able to do something else, like maybe work in an art store, where the employees weren't denigrated by the rest of society.

"Okay," Tim conceded. "Let's try someplace else. You pick."

They walked several more blocks down the highway before Marcie spotted a Mexican joint that didn't remind her of anywhere. They got a table, laughed, ate, played some pinball, and headed home.

"Can I put this in your fridge?" She held up her doggie bag containing her leftover burrito.

"For sure." Tim finished unlocking his door. Together, they stepped into the freezing cold.

"It's cold in here." She stepped closer to him.

"I can turn off the AC."

Feeling rebuffed, Marcie headed toward the fridge. And stepped in a cat dish. "Where's your cat?"

"Probably hiding under the bed." Tim opened a hall cupboard and took out fresh sheets.

"You don't have to change—"

"They need washin' anyway."

Marcie watched his scrawny but sexy body walk toward the bed and strip it before remaking it. Then he got another set of sheets and laid them out on the couch. "You don't have to sleep there," Marcie told him.

Tim grinned. "I thought about it, believe me, but I'm not ready."

"We don't have to have sex," Marcie offered, so Tim wouldn't have to explain what Pat had hinted at. "Or make any commitment." A dirty word to most men. At least, when she was involved. Then they ran off and made a commitment to somebody else. Which Tim would do if he wanted kids, though knowing ahead of time that he would leave would make letting go easier—when the time came. "We could just hold each other."

"Tempting, but my feelings'd get involved and that's what I'm not ready to deal with. I'm afraid I'd want to start drinkin' again, to feel nothin'."

"Aren't you on pills for that?"

"They're okay for the everyday stuff, but when you're close to somebody, it's too intense. I take on people's moods. Most normal people can keep out what's not theirs. Maybe it's what makes addicts unstable."

"But I'm happy being with you, and if I'm happy, then you'd be taking in a happy mood." Marcie beamed at her logic.

"It don't work like that. I'd just get freaked out worrying about the next part, 'cause the honeymoon never lasts."

"Why can't it? If both people want it to and work to make it happen."

"You sound like my therapist. It's hard to believe history won't repeat, especially when you look like my ex. Sorta like you not wanting to go into that restaurant, you know? Reminds you of something, don't it?"

"Yeah," she had to agree.

"So, see? You don't want to go there, to avoid it. Same as me. And you probably didn't choose to have those feelings, either, did you? They just came."

Marcie couldn't argue.

"When I look at you, yeah, I feel like I'm fallin' in love all over again, like when I first met my ex, but I don't know if it's with you or her, and I'm already feeling I'm headed down the same path, leading to the same drinking train wreck at the end, which I just can't go near. I get panicky, not happy."

"You're a different person now. You're not drinking, and I'm not her. And I didn't avoid restaurants completely, did I? I went into a different one. Both of us want to put our pasts behind us and start over. That gives us something in common we can go through together."

"Yeah, well, a woman who looks like my ex and triggers me wantin' to drink again ain't putting my past nowhere but right back in front of me. To me, that's not different."

"I don't want to drive you to drink," Marcie scoffed, feeling defeated. But she kept at him anyway. "We could take it slow." But what if she was like his ex? She didn't know what Tim's ex-wife was like. Didn't she, Marcie, always pick variations of the same man? Tim was just farther along a continuum; he'd quit drinking, though without leaving him in a better position, meaning he was more suitable for having a relationship with than her former choices. "You have to put your therapy into practice or it won't do any good."

"You wanna be the guinea pig?"

"Better than not having you."

"You can't be that desperate."

"I like you!"

"I know you do. I think you should see my therapist for your bad taste in men."

They laughed.

"You're fun. You're attractive," Marcie argued his good points.

"That's just the pills. The real me underneath's a mean, irritable, sarcastic, reclusive, nasty ass you wouldn't want to be around." He said it with a grin.

"But you are on pills," Marcie pointed out.

"They don't magically give me a personality, and I need to find out what that is."

"You won't discover it sitting around by yourself."

"It wouldn't be fair to you till I feel ready."

"It'd be a learning relationship. I know you want kids, so I know we won't be forever. Meanwhile, let me decide what's fair to me, 'cause I don' t know who I am in a relationship, either. All I've ever had are one-night's. So we could figure it out together."

"Yeah, well there's one big difference. You didn't wreck all your brain cells with alcohol and don't need pills to keep you in a decent mood. My therapist said I killed off all those cells that give people a sense of well-being.

Why I need medication, and I can't stay on it forever. As Pat mentioned, there's side effects."

"I said I don't care about that."

"I do. A man's gotta feel like a man. An' I don't wanna risk hurtin' nobody's feelings no more."

"I'd be hurt if you left now."

Tim shook out a sheet and laid it down on the couch. "A relationship has to be mutual. At the moment, I have nothing to offer."

"I'll wait."

Tim shook his head. "I don't need that kind of pressure. I just want to work, save for another house, and keep my emotions quiet. I hate feeling anxiety and that's what any emotion feels like to me right now."

"Which makes you feel like drinking," Marcie said, to show him she'd been listening. "If we just did fun things on weekends that didn't cost money till you got used to feeling certain emotions as positive . . ."

"Relationships shouldn't have limits."

"Good fences, good neighbours," Marcie argued.

"You don't give up, do you? And that's another thing, speakin' of neighbours. We live too damn close. I'd feel like I was under a microscope."

"I could ask the office if I could trade my suite for one on the other side of the property if a vacancy comes up."

Tim sighed. "You're tryin' too hard."

"How do you know you'll find someone who does want kids and when you're ready?"

"I always have."

And he was probably right. One thing she hated about men—they could just mentally snap their fingers and the right woman appeared.

"You're selling yourself short, wanting to get involved in a losing proposition. You can do better than me."

"What's better if I'm not interested? And what's the point if there aren't feelings?"

"Okay, what do I know?" Tim shrugged.

"I don't want to rip open your old wounds. I just think that both of us wanting each other and doing nothing about it is a waste."

Tim yawned. "I gotta work in the morning."

Meaning the discussion was over. The man in control again. What was left to say, anyway? Though there might still be some hope. If he didn't want her at all, he wouldn't have invited her to spend the night at his place. So, things might change.

"Stay up and watch some TV if you want. Trust me, I won't hear a thing once my pills kick in. In the morning, help yourself to coffee or whatever you can find in the cupboards. Just make sure you lock up when you leave. And don't let the cat out." Tim closed himself in the bathroom.

When he was done, she used it. While the toilet flushed, to mask any possible noise, she quietly opened his medicine cabinet . . . on a pharmacy! All four shelves were crammed with pill bottles. She took photographs, closed the door, washed, and went to his room, leaving the door open. Maybe after a night trip to the bathroom, if he needed one—which he should, with all the water he drank—he'd forget she was there and auto-pilot himself into his own bed, beside her. And if he did, he'd be mad at his mistake. At himself and at her, just for being there. Her tears fell on his pillow. Not how she imagined her first night in Florida. She should be happy. Ecstatic! Living her dream, instead of the same old shit in a different place.

Though, she supposed, being rejected by Tim was better than being Tim.

By morning, Tim hadn't climbed in with her, but his cat slept at the foot of the bed. Seven-fifty, read the lighted numerals on the night-table clock, the earliest she'd ever awakened without an alarm, and actually felt like getting up.

Trying not to disturb the cat, she reached down for her camera in her purse beside the bed and snapped a picture. Then, surprisingly full of energy, Marcie hopped in Tim's shower. After putting on makeup, she photographed the cat eating, wandering the living room, chasing bell toys she threw, and clawing the drapes. Perfect references for the new book illustrations.

At nine o'clock, when the office opened, she grabbed her suitcase, locked the door, and went down to pick up her key and sign the rental agreement. Along with her copy of it, the office ladies gave her a list of nearby amenities and a map of the area.

3. New Home

When Marcie opened her door, the same blast of freezing cold whooshed out at her. And her suite had the same stupid carpet as Tim's—in Florida, a hot place which regularly got flooded by hurricanes. Why didn't builders use tile or stone? At least she could change one thing. She shut off the AC and opened the patio door. She didn't come here to freeze. Then, so no one would see her suitcases out in plain view and slice through the mosquito screen to steal them, she took them into the bedroom to put in the closet and opened the door on a *walk-in* closet! The thing was the size of a room! Too bad she hadn't had one in Calgary, when she owned clothes. A waste here. Even if she stayed the rest of her life, a wardrobe of shorts, bikinis, and sundresses would never fill this one.

She locked up and walked to the bargain store. Once there, she loaded up a cart with an inflatable mattress, small kitchen appliances, dishes, and several bottles of diet pop—*soda* here—in flavours not available in Canada, like grape and cream soda. She printed her new digital photographs on an instant photo machine Canada didn't have either. A salesperson retrieved the patio chairs and a table she requested, which would, for now, be her furniture. Then she borrowed a cart to haul the goods home, deliciously warmed by the infusion of tropical air.

She poured herself a glass of very warm, diet grape soda, heated by the sun on the short trip, and put her items away, wishing she'd remembered to take her burrito out of Tim's fridge. But at least she'd have an excuse to go over tonight. Meanwhile, she'd need groceries. Before going to get some and returning the cart to the bargain store, she filled ice trays with water so she'd have ice in an hour or so.

An hour and a half later, after putting her groceries away and finishing half her deli sandwich, she changed into a bikini and brought a glass of cream soda with ice to the pool, which, with her own key, she ould access.

Bliss. She collapsed on a chaise longue and, tired from the day's errands, from the stress of the move, from fourteen years of way too much working, drifted off to the buzz of cicadas and passing bursts of loud music from cars entering the nearby gate.

Toward dinnertime, she showered, chose her best sundress, applied some light makeup, and walked over one breezeway and up Tim's flight of stairs. The sound of his TV filtered through his door as she knocked.

"Who is it?" a hostile voice demanded.

"Marcie," she meekly answered, regretting she'd come. He sounded in a bad mood. The irritable man he'd claimed he was without pills. They must have worn off, or he'd cut back in an attempt to wean himself off.

When he opened the door, he looked like he'd been woken up from a nap. One side of his face was all creased, half his hair stood on end, and his eyes blazed to kill.

"I'm sorry. I didn't know you'd be sleeping. Your TV was on and I, uh, left my burrito from last night in your fridge and thought . . ." Fur brushed her ankles. Marcie looked down at the escaping cat.

"Ah, *shit*." Tim charged out the door calling, "Nubbles! Get back here."

Now Tim had two reasons for hating her. Before going through the motions of helping him recover his pet—like she, in flip-flops, could run as fast as a cat—she retrieved her go-box, then joined Tim in his search.

So many leafy trees that Nubbles could have climbed. And bushes the cat could be hiding in. Cats liked fish.

Which meant Nubbles could have gone down to the duck pond, not knowing that a landlocked body of water probably wouldn't contain fish. Or Nubbles would be too scared of the big birds to go near the pond. Or the cat could have jumped over the wall.

Cats also liked chicken. Marcie opened her go-box and broke off a piece of burrito. "Here, Nubbles!" Nubbles's face appeared near the edge of a branch. When Tim held open his arms to catch the cat, Marcie shook the branch. At least Tim shouldn't be as mad at her now for losing his cat, since she'd also helped get it back. A neutralization of harm.

"You crazy kitty." Tim cuddled the fur ball in his arms, and Marcie found herself wishing she could feel those arms wrapped around her. "I see you got your burrito," he practically accused.

"Have you eaten?"

"Yeah." Tim climbed his stairs and closed his door, showing himself the opposite of the man she'd met last night. That instability he warned her of. Typical of addicts. Something she knew only too well. People happy when medicated on their substance of choice, miserable as all hell when they weren't. Did she want more of that? Never knowing who she'd be seeing, or when she'd be seeing him—supposing he'd agreed to see her at all?

Marcie dragged her feet home, stowed her go-box in the fridge, and plunked her ass on a plastic chair to stare out the patio window at the tops of palm trees silhouetted against the sunset as seen over the property's wall.

The whole evening loomed before her. So, she'd do what she'd come here to do. She took out the printed photographs of the poker players and sketched out several compositions before deciding which one she wanted to paint on a canvas. She also sketched out some of the cat, penciling in an unfolding story along with each illustration. Which made her think of Dennis and her promise to call him, but she didn't feel like going out to buy a phone now.

Around nine, figuring her new double-sized air mattress might need a couple hours to self-inflate, she spread it out, then unpacked and organized the contents of her suitcases onto closet shelves. That done, and when the mattress had filled, she opened her package of sheets and spread them out. No blankets here. She sighed with pleasure and, fully naked, climbed between the sheets at eleven o'clock. The second night in a row she'd hit the sack before her usual three or four a.m.

On the verge of sleep, a tickle on her leg wakened her, which she scratched, then drifted off into nightmares, back to the days of looking for her first job in Calgary. Doors slamming in her face. Greeks yelling. Her section of the restaurant filling up with demanding customers while her feet stayed frozen in place, rendering her unable to serve. People coming in and screaming orders she couldn't understand, while the cooks continued to make food and shoved it off the ledge of the pick-up window when she couldn't deliver it fast enough.

Drenched in sweat, she woke herself up to escape. Got a glass of water from the kitchen. Read some of the book she started on the plane. Then tried sleeping again.

This time, people left without paying. Older waitresses taunted, *You're too young; you're an idiot, don't you know that? Hurry up!* Then younger ones ridiculed, *You're too old to be doing this.* Men with over-white teeth leered in agreement while groping and tipping the younger girls.

Marcie woke up again and this time stayed up. It wasn't even dawn yet. She took her photos and a sketchbook onto her porch, flicked on the light, and sketched Tim's cat getting freaked by big birds. She caught a flash of Tim cycling past, likely heading to work. She hadn't seen him soon enough to say hi, and he hadn't acknowledged her either. He couldn't have missed her, sitting there with the light on, which meant he'd ignored her on purpose. Why did she keep falling for unavailable men?

When stores should be open, Marcie asked the office ladies if she could look in their business directory, found the address of an art store, and located it on her map.

Walking there would take half the day, but so what? She could enjoy Florida along the way. Wrapped in its delicious, hot, humid air, she photographed leaves larger than humans in the mess of roadside jungle. One of those giant purple birds she'd seen by the duck pond cruised past a few feet from her shoulders, appearing like a creature from the dinosaur age. She shot that. Almost every passing car honked as she trod along the pea-gravel shoulder of the highway, sparkling with broken glass. More than one bag of fast-food trash—not garbage—got pitched from an open car window into the ditch, already half-full of litter. Environmentalism hadn't made its way south.

She stopped for coffee and the best bagel ever, listening to brown people speak Spanish.

The art store, when she finally arrived, was huge, and everything was so cheap. She loaded a cart with more canvases, brushes, extra sketchbooks, and paints than she could carry, which was fine, because she wasn't walking all that way home anyway, over-laden *or* empty-handed. She asked the cashier to call her a cab, thinking to herself that she really needed to buy a phone.

Once home, more tired than hungry, she dumped her supplies in the living room, changed into her bikini, and napped by the pool in the late afternoon sun, without nightmares, until woken by dark. She went in, made and ate dinner, organized her supplies around an empty dining room, and paint-mapped poker players on canvas.

In the morning, after more nasty restaurant dreams and breakfast, Marcie brought her poker canvas out to the pool to start painting, before falling asleep mid-afternoon. This time, a shadow woke her.

"You must be Marcie," its voice spoke. A woman with bouffant black hair and wide hips blocked the sun. "I'm Chrissy, Ken's girlfriend. You met him the other night when he was passing through the pool on his way home."

Passing through?

"Watcha painting?" Chrissy's eyes popped, soon after she grabbed the canvas. She then snatched the photographs to verify who she thought she saw. "That lying piece of shit!" Chrissy furiously leafed through snapshots of evidence. "He said he quit playin' poker! He was supposed to have been out looking for a job. I'm tired of supporting his ass. My settlement money was supposed to be for our vacation. I swear I'll throw him out before I cover one more of his gambling debts! His friends never pay us—*like that* little weasel." A red salon nail stabbed at the Hispanic guy who'd run off. Chrissy tossed the photographs back on the table then reached in her purse. With as much venom, she poked at the keys of her cell phone then held it to her ear while she waited. "No shit he's not answering."

She threw the phone back in her purse and stomped off on spongy wedge heels.

A man Marcie hadn't even slept with and she'd still gotten him into trouble.

Marcie painted until her stomach rumbled past the point of toleration, then packed up. While she unlocked her door, Jim, the shorter Black man from the poker game, emerged from his suite across the breezeway.

"Let's see." He examined the painting of the poker players. His expression quickly changed from a patronizing smile to amazement. "*Holy shit*! You're good!"

"It's not finished."

"I want it when it is. How much?"

"I don't know. Three hundred?"

Jim peeled three hundreds off a roll he took from his pocket. "Put all that shit away and come over for beer and pizza. There's some guys here from work."

Why not? Maybe she'd meet someone to help her forget Tim. Now that he wasn't even speaking to her. And he didn't want her to wait.

"No need to put any clothes on," Jim called.

"Unless your AC's been off, there is."

Marcie threw on a sundress and sweater before entering Jim's; he'd left the door open. The place reeked like pot, cigarettes, and stale beer. Latino reggae blasted from the speakers.

"Hellooo, pretty lady," an extremely tall Black man greeted her. "Jim wasn't kidding." He shoved the man beside him farther away and patted the small, now-empty space on the couch beside him. The man who'd been shoved aside reached across the man who'd displaced him for a pizza slice from a box balanced on a stack of magazines on the coffee table. Cans of beer and ashtrays surrounded the precarious tower.

"Excuse their manners," Jim interceded. "They're labour."

"At least we work. He sits on his ass, obviously." The guy patted Jim's stomach.

"Like turning the steering wheel on a baggage cart's such a big physical effort," Jim shot back.

"Yeah, well, them bags don't load themselves in and out of the cargo bays." The guy tilted his head back to sword-swallow a whole slice of cheesy pepperoni, causing, via over-extended elbow, the guy beside him to knock a heaping ashtray off the table onto the dingy orange shag carpeting.

"Hey. Look what you did."

A guy in the process of setting down his beer looked and missed the table, spilling some beer and creating a small, ash-topped lake on the carpet.

"Now you know why goods get damaged in transport." Jim lumbered off and returned with a towel.

As Marcie helped herself to a slice, she noticed Abe, passed out on a chair, bathed in a diamond pattern of lamplight because of the way a net shirt was draped over the lampshade, making him look almost angelic. If she could capture that image on canvas . . . She plucked her camera out of her purse.

"Are you, like, a photographer?"

"She's an artist," Jim explained. "I just bought one of her paintings. And, she illustrated a children's book."

"Then why you takin' a picture a him? Kids don't need to see that shit. No one does. Now, if you could catch him awake, that'd be worth recording on film." He swigged what was left of his beer.

"Cameras don't use film no more, idiot," one of his co-workers informed him. "It's all digital."

"Whatever. So are you, like, famous?"

"No." Marcie put her camera away after perfectly capturing Abe and picked up her pizza.

"Yeah, right. Then how come you can afford to come all the way down here from Canada and not work?"

Word travelled.

"Can you paint *me*?" He opened his shirt on an eight pack. "I look better than he does. An'"—he softened his voice and grinned a mouthful of white teeth—"it gets better further down."

"If you got a magnifying glass," Jim added disdainfully.

A flash of movement past the crack in the drapes caught her attention. Tim riding by, this time home from work, on his bicycle. She noted the time, so tomorrow she could maybe happen to be out sketching something by the gate, where he'd see her and couldn't ignore her. Though, why stalk a recovering addict who'd said no in plain New Jersey English and hated her for waking him up from a nap and letting his cat escape? To apologize. So they could be at least friendly, if not friends. In order to, what, keep some stupid hope alive? Maybe she *should* go see his therapist. Marcie reached for another beer. Maybe, if she drank enough, she could quiet her fantasies, like Tim had tried numbing his feelings.

Around midnight, she left with everyone else, but— preferring not to face more nightmares— instead of going to bed, she stayed up to work on her painting of the poker players. Then she slept away the morning by the pool.

At noon, she headed to the grocery store for some things she hadn't realized she needed. Having always eaten out, either at work or at friends' work, shopping for food wasn't something she'd ever been used to.

"Hey, cart lady!" called a familiar voice behind her, as she grabbed a cart.

"Not at work?" Marcie questioned Pat.

"Not on Saturday. Though why would you know what day it was?" Pat followed her in but didn't grab a cart for himself.

"Are we sharing?"

"I just came in to get headache pills," Pat explained. "When I was married, I never used to drink like this. Being single sucks. What'd you do all day, paint?" He pointed to the paint on her arms.

Marcie looked at them. "Oh. Yeah."

"How was your night with Tim?"

"I wouldn't say I spent it *with Tim*. He slept on the couch."

"All I needed to know." Pat grinned. "How about spending tonight with me? I bet you don't have a bed yet."

"Actually, I bought an inflatable mattress."

"It should hold both of us. You know I'm in love with you."

"I don't feel the same way." Marcie set him straight.

"Yeah, you want Tim."

"And he wants his ex."

"You just can't win. Love stinks. Remember that song from the eighties?"

"Yup. Sums up my whole life."

"You never been married?" Pat asked, astonished. "Though if Tim's any indication of your taste in men, no wonder."

"Yeah, well, I wish I could control my heart, too. But I can't. And I can't be with somebody if my heart's with somebody else."

"You should try." Pat grabbed a pill bottle, knowing exactly what brand he preferred.

"Why'd you and your wife separate?"

"She wants kids. And when we found out I was the one firing blanks, she started sleeping around. No way in hell was I payin' to raise some other man's kid, so I left before she got pregnant."

"Smart. But you should still get divorced, or you could still end up paying."

"Yeah. I've been puttin' it off."

Pat trolled the aisles with her as she loaded her cart and helped her carry her bags to her door. Marcie looked at her watch.

"He doesn't get home till at least five-thirty, if you're worried about him seeing us together."

"We aren't together." Marcie reminded Pat, as she unlocked her door.

"Phew, it's hot in here!"

"I shut off the AC." Marcie slid back the patio door for fresh air.

"I hope you don't leave that open at night."

"Why? With the wall and the locked gate? Should I worry?"

"Not about burglars."

"Then what?"

Pat looked around the floor and up the walls.

"What aren't you guys telling me?"

"So, you want kids?" Pat asked.

"No. But that doesn't mean we're soul mates. And you changed the subject."

"Sexually, we'd be perfect. Birth control pills aren't good for women. With me, you could go off 'em."

"I'm not on them. I had my tubes tied."

"Tim wants kids."

"I know. The man who's too afraid of his own feelings and can't handle anyone else's wants a family. How dumb is that?"

"That's addicts for you. Always have their heads in a cloud. Plus, with the drinking he's done and the pills he's on now, any kid of his'll likely be born with some kind of problem."

"No kidding. Convince him of that."

"I'd rather not do you that favour. And I'd bet, with all the woman he's had, he's probably got kids already. Maybe from when he was healthier. Hell, a few more years, they'll be bangin' on his door, wanting to meet their real dad." Pat shook his head and rubbed his thumb and fingers together to indicate those kids would want money. "You want to be stuck with somebody facing so many potential lawsuits for backlogged child support? The guy's a zero and women are all over him. All you guys see are his teeth and blond hair." Pat grabbed Marcie's sunglasses off the counter and slapped them on his face while flashing his teeth in a comic imitation of Tim. "Dumbass looks like a magazine ad."

Marcie giggled and started putting the groceries away.

Pat removed the glasses and tossed them back where they'd been. "I don't get it. He's got the same skin-and-bones body I do, yet every female loses her mind over him."

"Love isn't logical, though maybe bankers think it should be."

"I'm not a banker. I'm a voice thug in a suit, with an office in a bank. And I hate it. Trying to intimidate people into paying their bills."

"Then why don't you look for something else?"

"It has medical and pays pretty good."

Marcie balled up the empty plastic bags and tossed them under the sink where she kept her garbage can. Trash can.

"Think about this. If you can't make a living at being an artist and don't want to go back to work, or to Canada, marry me and you wouldn't have to do either. You could sit around all day and paint. Even if you don't love me right away and we just got along, that'd be all right. Love can grow, and there's something to be said for good company. I'd even quit drinking."

Pat sounded as desperate as she did, pitching herself to Tim. "For me, there's gotta be passion. You know, that something that surges inside when you look at someone?"

"Maybe that's why you have shit luck with men," Pat proposed. "Listenin' too much to stupid hormones."

"That's what Tim said." Marcie glanced at her watch.

"Okay, time to go. I get it. Getting on to five-thirty." Pat wrote out his phone number on the back of the grocery slip. Another reminder to get a phone.

As soon as Pat left, she grabbed her sketchbook and pencil crayons and sat by the gate to sketch a palm tree as a pretense for being there. At 5:33, she caught sight of Tim's blond hair above the lane's hedge. Her heart sped. "Tim!" she feigned surprise when he opened the gate.

"Hey, Marcie," he acknowledged politely.

"Just getting off work?"

"Yeah. Hard day. Look, I'm really sorry for snappin' at ya the other night. I slept through my pill time. It wasn't your fault the cat got out. I was tired and irritable and should have seen her sooner."

"No worries. I was going to apologize too for bothering you. I'm glad you got her back. Hey, have you had dinner?"

"I'm not very entertaining after work. I was just gonna grab a barbecued chicken after I showered and watch some TV."

"Why don't I pick one up while you shower, and I can watch TV with you! It's the weekend," Marcie reminded him, not that he'd agreed to her proposed weekends-only deal.

"If you want," Tim gave in. "Here." He reached in his pocket and gave her a bill. "You ain't workin'."

Marcie's heart soared, and not because he was paying—he'd agreed to spend an evening with her!

"I'll leave my door unlocked. Just come in."

The heat of anticipation spread through her body as she dumped her art supplies inside her apartment, ran out for a chicken and salad, then showered and changed.

Opening Tim's door, she found him passed out on the couch, still wearing his work clothes. This time, she wasn't waking him up. The smell of the chicken could do it itself, or not. It got the attention of Nubbles. Marcie carried the bags to the kitchen, forked a portion of chicken into a dish and set it on the floor.

Half an hour passed. Then an hour. Still, Tim snored. Should she wait? What if he didn't wake up until morning? She remembered how tired she used to get after a week of long shifts, when she'd collapse for thirteen-plus hours, but not if she had a date. Maybe that was the difference between being on medication and not. Or being in love and not.

Hungry, Marcie quietly searched Tim's cupboards for a plate, hacked off some chicken, dished out some salad, and ate while watching Tim flopped out on the couch with his eyes closed. A sample of what life with him would be like. She could lie down beside him right now and drape his arms over her, and he likely wouldn't notice, though what pleasure could come from that? And he might be mad when he woke up, finding her all snuggled into him and having missed a pill. So, she stayed at his dining table, though he could still be ticked to find her there, too, because she'd remained in his apartment for too long, when she should have figured out he obviously wasn't waking up, and left. Had he *wanted* this to happen, so she could see and experience what life with him would be like and, thus, go away? Permanently? Or had he wanted to spend the evening with her but his body, perpetually drugged out on pharma meds and exhausted from work, independently behaved otherwise?

At nine o'clock, far beyond any reasonable length of time to wait, she wrote a note on the paper bag that the chicken had been in, saying she'd been there and that the rest of the chicken and salad were in the fridge. If she had a phone, she could have left her number. So instead she scribbled, *Drop by anytime.* Then put the note, along with his change, on the coffee table, and let herself out, watching for Nubbles, and locking the door behind her.

Tears of disappointment welled up on the short walk home. She was in love with a shell. A fantasy of her own making, which didn't exist. It was the pattern of her whole life. Nothing she hoped for ever happened except what she could make happen herself. Like painting, quitting waitressing, and moving to Florida. But her dream alone wasn't making her happy. More than anything, she wanted someone. Not anyone, or she could have Pat. But someone *she* wanted. Why did she have to want Tim?

She opened her door . . . and saw a black spot on the carpet. In a place she didn't paint. Odd. She hadn't seen it before. How could she have missed something so obvious? Hopefully, it'd come out. She walked to the kitchen for a paper towel, wet it, and sprayed it with cleaner, but when she turned around, the spot was gone! Or rather, had moved! Because it was now close to the wall! Impossible! She wiped at her eyes and approached and saw the black thing had wings! And legs! And antennae! Like some kind of Satanic butterfly! She continued to stare at it in horror, wondering what she should do. She couldn't leave it there, but she couldn't step on it, either, or its goo would be ground into the carpet. Would it jump if she tried catching it? Did it sting? Maybe she could capture it in something and take it outside or drown it. She got a glass and a piece of stiff sketching paper, then dropped the glass over it like a dome and slid the paper underneath. She then carried her trap to the bathtub and let the pressure of the water wash the creepy thing down the drain.

Too shaky to paint, she read until she got tired enough to try going to sleep, yet she was afraid of sleeping, too, because of the dreams. She couldn't escape being a waitress.

After finishing *Poker Players* Sunday morning, she took the painting over to Jim. Thrilled, he hung it up on his wall right away. Marcie stared down at the stack of magazines. Porn, mostly. Some sports. More subjects to draw from. "You want those? Take 'em all," Jim offered.

Marcie carted the pile home to leaf through later, then set up her usual paint camp by the pool, where she worked on Abe bathed in light diamonds.

The whole day, she remained the only one by the pool. What was wrong with Floridians that they didn't want to be outside?

Needing some exercise late in the day, she went for a walk. Then ate dinner. Then leafed through her magazines, cutting out pictures she'd like to paint, remembering too late she could have bought a phone while she was out. If she had one, she could have called Pat. For the company. She wasn't used to spending so much time alone. Jim's place was dark, so she couldn't go over there. Blue TV light glowed from Tim's windows, but she wasn't bothering Tim. Not after he fell asleep on her last night. He had to come to her now, and if he didn't, that might be a message to listen to.

"You're doin' more sleeping than painting." Chrissy's harsh voice woke Marcie from a poolside nap the next afternoon.

"I get nightmares at night and can't sleep."

Chrissy stared at the canvas of Abe. "I don't know how, but you're making that scumbag look like a saint. I should get you to paint Ken. Seein' himself in a higher light might inspire him to reach for something other than improving his poker game. Since you're not doing anything, why don't you come for a ride? I got errands in Clearwater."

Why not? Marcie gathered up her supplies. Chrissy picked up the canvas and followed Marcie to her apartment. "Geez, it's hot in here. And you don't have any furniture!"

"I just got here."

"Yeah, but you didn't *bring* anything?"

"Some clothes. Shipping's too expensive from Canada. Once I know I can earn a living here and stay, I'll buy furniture. But why, when I'm by the pool all day anyway?"

"Yeah, well, winter's coming. You won't be by the pool then."

"Winter? What, the temperature's going to drop to seventy-something?" Marcie joked.

"You Canadians don't know shit about Florida. You think the weather's great, so you come down here, buy up all the real estate, and drive the prices sky-high so we can't afford homes, then complain all through hurricane season and when it gets cold around Christmas."

"In Canada, we have overseas people doing the same thing. But, if it makes you feel better, I can't afford a house in either place, and our hurricanes come in the winter. We call 'em blizzards."

"Ken said you illustrated a children's book."

"Yeah. You want to look at it while I shower?" Marcie handed Chrissy a copy.

"It's cute," Chrissy commented, when Marcie returned to the living room, cleaned up and ready to go. "So are you, like, famous?"

"No." Marcie grabbed her purse and followed Chrissy across the property to another parking lot where she unlocked a red sports car. "Nice."

"I bought it secondhand with part of my insurance settlement."

Marcie got in and buckled her seatbelt. Chrissy cruised around the loop road surrounding the property inside the wall and exited the front gate.

"Ken wants me to sell it, so he can use the money to pay his gambling debts and give us more disposable income for him to dispose of. I'll throw him out first."

Chrissy turned down the lane and barged in front of an oncoming car. Brakes squealed, metal collided, glass broke, and men hollered behind them.

Marcie whipped her head around to look at the wreckage. "Shouldn't you stop?" Marcie asked.

"Why? I didn't hit nobody. Nobody hit me."

"A guy just rear-ended the guy behind you."

"That's their problem. And I didn't see it, so what's the point of hanging around, waitin' for the cops to come, which might never happen?"

"What if the guy who got rear-ended because of you takes your licence plate number?"

"So he does. And why would he care? 'Cause he'll get money from the guy who hit him from behind."

Marcie's mouth dropped.

"It's not my fault he was driving too fast and had to slam on his brakes or if the guy behind him was following too close."

Marcie closed her mouth and said nothing further, but watched the road nervously, like that could prevent Chrissy from doing anything else stupid. Like cutting across three lanes of traffic to get in the left turn lane, then pulling a U-ie around the boulevard! And she was deemed to be not at fault for her last accident? Now wanting to go right, she stuffed the car into the right lane, using only her mirrors to check if she had space. What if a car had been directly beside her? She then merged onto an eight-lane highway.

"You look nervous." Chrissy studied Marcie.

Watch the road, Marcie telepathed.

"Are you criticizin' my driving?"

"I didn't say a thing."

"But you thought it. You Canadians are deceitful. You never say what's in your head."

"A lot of Canadians think Americans are rude because you say whatever's in yours without thinking how anybody'll feel."

"Then you guys's skin is too thin if you can't handle some honest truth. We call a dumbass a dumbass. At least with us, you don't have to worry about where you stand or what we're thinking. We say what we think to your face. You Canadians just stab each other in the back while smiling like nothin's wrong."

What could she say? Because to a point that was true. Only Canadians heard the unspoken. "Watch . . ." Marcie pointed at a car cutting over a few lanes, likely to exit. Did they all drive like that here? Hence the number of lawyers, all advertising their services on billboards and on every white page of the phone book.

"I see him." Chrissy touched the brakes in time to avoid getting clipped, which probably would have flipped their car and a few others. "Idiot. Don't know where he's goin'."

"You did the same thing a while back," Marcie heard her voice remind Chrissy, free of the constraints of having to be nice to customers.

Chrissy gasped.

"You just said you liked people to say what they're thinking, so I did. And if you really want me to be honest, I don't know how *you* got the insurance settlement."

"Look. If you don't like the way I drive, you can get out of the car."

"Pull over, I will."

"Are you serious? You want out on the Veterans Expressway?"

"It was your idea."

Chrissy chomped aggressively on her gum. "You Canadians are such chicken shits. You won't go to war but are always telling us what we should do. Get out of Iraq. Have government-paid health care. Spend less on the military and more on social programs. Yet you guys never get off your asses and do anything about the *evil* in the world. Like Vietnam, or Saddam Hussein, or the Taliban, or the spread of communism. But you sure as hell enjoy the freedom our boys give their lives for and we give our tax dollars to."

Marcie blinked.

"You don't know shit, either, about what's going on in the world. Just stick your heads in the sand. That way you can keep your prissy noses clean and absolve yourself from gettin' involved."

"I thought you wanted me to get out."

Chrissy finally slowed to a stop on the shoulder.

"If you hate Canadians so much, why'd you even ask me to come?" Marcie lifted the handle of the door to open it, but it stayed locked. She looked over at Chrissy, who then clicked off the auto-lock. Marcie shouldered open the car door.

"Now you can run away like the chicken shit alla y'all are."

The instant Marcie slammed the door shut, the tires spit small stones and bits of glass into her shins and ankles. She watched as the car accelerated and Chrissy forced her way back into traffic, causing a chain of brake lights to go on. *Psychopath!*

Now, standing on the shoulder, Marcie wished she hadn't put off getting a cell phone. Though what would she do? Call a cab and say she was someplace a few miles out of town on the Veterans Expressway? She didn't even know if it ran east-west or north-south, or which side she was on. For sure, dispatch would get right on sending a car, and if one *did* come, the driver would have to keep heading in whatever direction the road was going until the next exit, then turn around and come back. Which would be very expensive.

She could turn around and walk. She had the time, but should she do it without water, in this heat? Or, she could cross eight lanes of speeding traffic and attempt to hitch-hike. Fat chance she'd make it, since any time the stream of cars let up in one direction, they kept ripping past from the other. The narrow barricade dividing the freeway wasn't wide enough to comfortably stand on to wait. So, she'd hitch-hike in the direction she faced. Why not see Clearwater? She had the whole day. And the next one. And the day after that, for the next six months at least. When she was ready, she could hitch another ride back.

Marcie turned around and stuck out her thumb. Practically as soon as she faced the on-coming traffic, a car stopped.

"Where're ya headed?" the driver asked.

"Wherever you're going is fine."

"You okay?"

"Fine."

"You're not in any kind of trouble, are you?"

"No."

"It's just unusual to pick up somebody who has no destination in mind. And no luggage."

"I was going to Clearwater with my friend, but we had a fight."

"So he dumped you on the Veterans Expressway?"

"*She* asked if I wanted out of the car. I took her up on it."

The man laughed, his concern dispelled. "So not a relationship *friend*," he clarified.

"No. More an acquaintance from my apartment-home complex."

He smiled. "Well, great. Clearwater's where I'm going. I'm Stan," he introduced himself.

"Marcie."

"Nice to meet you. You Canadian?"

"My accent?"

"A dead giveaway." Stan grinned.

"You don't sound like you're from around here, either."

"California. I'm travelling on business."

"Oh. What do you do?"

"Computer consultant."

"Oh."

"And you?"

"I saved some money and illustrated a children's book, so I came down here to see how long I can last, scamming an existence as an artist."

"Are you famous?" Stan grinned.

"No."

"You got a website?"

"I don't even know what that is."

"It's like an online store. I can make you one. Then you can attract buyers from all over the world."

"I don't even have a computer."

"You can buy computer time at a copy place or internet cafe. Cheap. Like a couple bucks an hour. I'd love to see some of your work. And I bet my kids would love a copy of your book."

"I happen to have one. And I have my recent work on my camera, though the only finished piece I have here already sold."

"Maybe we could have dinner."

"Sure." She'd sleep with him for a website. If that's what he wanted. Or maybe he was just being nice. Bored on the road and wanted someone to talk to. Like she was bored, spending so much time alone. Because, why else would she have agreed to go to Clearwater with Chrissy?

"I have a client to see first." Stan signalled to exit and sanely did so, turning onto a much quieter road with water on both sides, narrow beaches, and lots of palm trees. Paradise plus.

"Wow," Marcie gasped, gazing out the window.

"Wanna stop? I have time."

"Sure."

After Stan parked his van, they stepped over a wood fence onto some stones. Marcie sat, then reverently pointed her camera at a seamless horizon, right around where the powder blue sky melded with the same colour water. Literally, the picture of calm. "It's so peaceful," she whispered.

"I love this stretch. Maybe there's another way to Clearwater, but this is how I always go whenever I get a call to the Bay Area."

Stan sat down close to her, where they stayed shoulder to shoulder staring out at the sea until he kissed her, then said they should get going.

On entering Clearwater, Stan pointed to a huge bridge under construction beside the smaller, lower one they were about to drive across. "See how those two sides don't meet in the middle?" He shook his head. "This used to be a great country. Now we can't even build a damn bridge. And our foreign policy?" Stan shook his head. "I won't even go into that. But the taxpayers are gonna end up stuck with this bill, yet again eating into money that should be going toward education. Always an excuse for cuts. The dumbing of America." Stan snorted cynically. "We have to import engineers. And still . . ." He pointed to the gap in the bridge.

He drove for a while, then let her out at the beach. "You got a cell phone?"

"No."

"Then how 'bout we meet at Gilligan's at five o'clock. It's right there on the beach." He pointed to a straw roof. "If something goes wrong, you should be able to find a payphone somewhere to call me." He gave her his card. "Looking forward."

"Me too." Marcie slid out of the car.

Stan was different, unlike her typical type. He'd show up for their date and not get sidetracked with another woman or more work, nor end up too drunk during an afternoon of business; she could feel it. And he didn't have a problem with guilt, like most sober married men. Which he assumed he was since he mentioned having kids, but he might not be. Married. She might learn something about how a decent relationship should be, even if theirs never went further than dinner or the next morning. Already, they were talking, and not just as friends. The kiss promised something more.

Marcie walked toward the ocean. Or, rather, the Gulf. The air felt charged with an exciting potential and expectation that something could happen. Something had. She was here, in Florida, at a beach, mid-September, and had a dinner date with a man she was somewhat attracted to, though not at Tim level. Time to settle for less. Because Tim was right. When the same-old wasn't working, explore something new.

As she walked along the sand, she noticed a gorgeous lifeguard sitting high up in a chair, his tanned and oiled muscles glistening in the sun. That guy could make her forget Tim, though what were the odds a guy like that wouldn't have a girlfriend, or one not completely filling the bill? With his looks, he'd get whoever he wanted. But even if she did stand a chance, why start something with somebody in a place twenty miles away? Though, if he had a car, twenty miles wasn't that far. But still, she could walk in front of his chair and, what, hope he'd look at her? Hard, though, to tell through his reflective sunglasses exactly where he was looking. And what would she say? Because he wasn't likely to talk to her first, and with no bathing suit, she couldn't exactly swim out and call for help.

Why weren't people swimming? The ones who'd planned to come to the beach and wore bathing suits. Water was never too cold for kids, and the beach was full of them, digging in the sand and chasing each other around. So what, all these moms irrationally feared rip tides or drop-offs which could potentially snatch away toddlers? And if the water really was too dangerous for swimming, why would there be a lifeguard? And Chrissy accused Canadians of being cowards. Unless these were Canadian tourists. Though Canadians, maybe hesitant about speaking their minds, generally weren't afraid of the water.

Marcie took off her flip-flops to feel the sand on her feet and was about to wade in when a voice from above yelled, "Hey!" So, she'd gotten the lifeguard's attention, but, judging from his tone, not in a positive way. Was his purpose to keep people out of the water? Then why wasn't a sign posted? And how far out did it look like she'd go, wearing a dress and carrying a purse! Puzzled and mildly irritated, Marcie put on a neutral expression and looked upward.

"Yeah, you!"

"What, I didn't shower before entering?" Marcie joked.

"Don't you read?"

"There's a sign?"

"Yeah." He pointed down the beach in the opposite direction she'd come from. "Sharks."

"Seriously? But I'm not going swimming." Marcie pointed to her dress—not a bathing costume. "Just wading. Maybe up to my knees."

"You're not from here, are you?"

That again. "No."

"Sharks like the surf."

"So you're telling me a shark is going to swim up to the beach in a couple feet of water and chomp off my ankles?"

"Basically, yeah. That's where they feed."

That wasn't what happened in *Jaws*.

"We saw sharks this morning. That's why we posted the shark warning."

"Oh." Marcie edged away from the water and walked off. Okay, forget him. He'd treated her like a stupid kid, or an idiot tourist. Not a turn-on. She snapped a picture of the beach and of him. Let him yell at her for that.

Marcie found a spot on the sand in front of Gilligan's so she wouldn't have to worry about being late to meet Stan if she fell asleep, her afternoon habit. Stan would see her passed out on the sand if she didn't wake up before five.

But she did. Her good old sense of timing, which always woke her when she napped between shifts when she used to work splits.

Very badly needing to pee, she brushed off the sand and headed toward Gilligan's, entering at four fifty-eight. Stan was already sitting on the patio, smiling, and sipping one of two slushy lime drinks. Marcie waved. "I'm joining him," she informed the hostess, a girl in a bikini bra and a grass skirt. "But first, where's your washroom?" She held up a finger to Stan, indicating she'd be back in a minute.

"I'm glad you came." Stan stood to greet and kiss her as she approached his table.

Like he wasn't sure if she'd show. Yet he'd ordered two drinks.

"Cheers!" he lifted his.

She picked up hers and clinked for the toast. "How was your meeting?" Which sounded very domestic. Something a wife might ask a husband, not typical first-date conversation. He comfortably answered—not all defensive, like she was invading his privacy. Without going into too much technical detail she wouldn't understand anyway, he gave her a brief rundown of his day. Then he asked, "How was the beach?"

"Full of sharks, apparently. Is that true? That they swim that closet to shore?"

"Oh, yeah."

"Well. Good to know." She stared out at the open water, feeling like she was on a TV set. "You watch *Gilligan's Island* when you were a kid?"

"All the time. We used to string hammocks up on the beach and pretend we were castaways. You want to see where I grew up?" He unfolded a laptop and typed, which called up a magnificent picture of a stunning cliff with rocks and seals at its base against an ocean backdrop. "Northern California. In the summer, we used to drive up the coast to the Oregon dunes." He typed again and called up pictures of giant sand dunes as tall as phone poles. Marcie gasped. "Yeah, you can go on virtual tours of anywhere. What do you wanna see? Paris? Vegas? The pyramids?"

He surfed around from place to place, like a man with a remote control for the TV. Now Marcie wished she could travel.

"You've never poked around on the internet?"

Not something waitresses did. "The only computers I've ever used were point-of-sale systems and I hated those. Half the time, they don't let you do what you want, and if they do, it takes three times as long as just writing it down on a piece of paper."

"That's part of what I do. Making systems more user-friendly. And it's kind of new technology so it'll be a while before we work all the bugs out."

A waitress dressed like the hostess asked if they were ready to order.

"Guess we should look at the menus." Stan opened his and asked if she wanted to share a seafood combo.

"Perfect." From her experience, the size of one meal here fed two.

"We'll have to set you up with an email account. That way we can keep in touch."

Something she needed to do so she could send her cat drawings to Dennis.

Stan typed. "You'll be able to access it from anywhere; you just have to sign in. What do you want your address to be?"

"Sharks on the beach?"

Stan turned his screen so she could see and typed in sharksonthebeach. "Now enter a password." Stan looked away.

A whole new world had emerged while she'd been in the bar helping people escape from theirs.

As their server approached with their food, Stan snapped shut his laptop and slid it back in its briefcase. "Dig in!"

But something ate at her stomach. "So who's going to want hand-painted pictures when there're all those images people can print off and frame?"

"That's why they will. To be different. You paint unique originals."

"You haven't seen them. I'm a realist."

"Still. They'll have your own special touch. Something of value people can get only from you."

Before her hands got all greasy, Marcie pulled out her camera and showed Stan her work.

"That's amazing! Look at the detail! This is good!" Stan zoomed in.

While he looked, Marcie grabbed his pen and drew a sketch of him on the back of her placemat.

"Hey!" Stan noticed, delighted.

"A memento." She presented the simple image of himself, captured in just a few lines.

"You have a talent. You should set up on a beach or someplace and do that. People'll pay good money for quality portraits. Just think what you could do with a pencil and colour."

"Yeah?" Something she hadn't thought of.

"Go sit down near Channelside, where the cruise ships dock. The tourists'll eat it up."

Marcie pulled out *Dodger the Dog*. "This is my children's book."

Stan flipped through the pictures. "These are great."

"For you."

"Thanks. My kids'll love this. Okay, let's eat."

Stan dropped the book in his briefcase and returned Marcie's camera. She dropped it in her purse and picked up a prawn.

When they finished, the waitress cleared their plates and offered dessert.

After paying what he called *the check*, not *the bill,* they walked along the beach into the sunset, something she'd always wanted to do with a man. "Don't put your feet in the water," Marcie teased.

"How many surfers does it take to change a light bulb?" Stan asked.

Marcie shrugged.

"They can't. The sharks have chewed off their arms."

"They're that bad?"

"Hell, yeah. You just never hear about it or it'd scare off the tourists. So, I'm headed back to Tampa tomorrow morning, if you want a ride. But that'd mean you'd have to spend the night in my room." Stan put his soft arms around her and kissed her. He didn't have the hard body she was used to, but she liked him. She kissed him back and they walked hand in hand to his room on the third floor of a five-star hotel, overlooking a lit-up garden of palms surrounding a swimming pool in the shape of a kidney bean.

"First, let's make that website." Stan opened his laptop. "And then I'll show you how to upload more photos."

Once virtual business was finished, they adjourned to the pool, where they shared a chaise and stared into the night. Paradise just kept getting better. She photographed it. Then, after a quick dip in water not infested with anything more threatening than chlorine and possibly child's pee, they went back to the room, shared a shower, and enjoyed hours of languid sex. Not the desperate, breathtaking, clawing, screaming kind that left both people spent in ten minutes; this felt different. But it would lead to the same thing, or almost: a goodbye in the morning. Connected by email, Marcie supposed they might see each other again. Stan travelled. If he paid, Marcie could travel.

In the morning, she took more photographs as they ate breakfast in a rainforest setting, complete with live parrots.

When Stan let her off at the front gate of her apartment complex, he thanked her for an amazing time. She thanked him for the same thing, plus dinner, email, and website.

"Keep in touch." He kissed her. "You still have my card?" he confirmed. "I'll let you know when I'm back through this way again. I really enjoyed meeting you."

Maybe he'd get a divorce. But that would make her a stepmother. To six kids. She might rather freeze her ass back in Canada and wait tables. "Me too," she could honestly say. Just to meeting him and seeing him again, not a future. Though their time together was short, Stan had served as a genuine teaching relationship which she felt had broken a pattern. What she'd offered to Tim. Though she had nothing to teach. And he'd probably sensed that.

"Are you just getting home?" Ken stood beside the gate, smoking. Not a relaxing morning smoke, but an uptight one. Like some disaster had happened.

"Yeah."

"Fuck, we were going to call the police. Chrissy said she went back to look for you, and you were gone."

"If I wanted out of her car in the first place, why would she expect I'd wait for her so I could get back in?"

"Where'd you go?"

"Clearwater."

"You walked?"

"Hitch-hiked."

Which, judging from Ken's eyes, he seemed to think worse. "Are you crazy? You could have been killed."

"That's what I was afraid of if I'd stayed in the car!"

Ken suddenly smirked, then lit up like a Christmas tree. "Seriously? Wait'll I tell her." He almost bolted off.

"She should know. I told her myself."

"She told me you couldn't take talking politics." Ken flicked away his half-finished cigarette. Something nobody in Canada did. Not at eleven dollars a pack. People smoked right down to the filter. "By the way, thanks for busting me. Can I at least see this painting?"

"Jim has it. But I'll show you a photograph of it if you want. Right after I pee."

Ken followed her into her apartment. "Fuck, it's hot in here. You got the AC off?"

"Is there a rule against that? A sign somewhere I didn't see?" Marcie snapped.

"In rentals, yeah. It's in your lease. All apartments have to be kept at eighty degrees or colder 'cause of mold.

If you get evicted over that, good luck getting another place." He looked around. "You don't have any furniture."

"Yeah, I know." Marcie acknowledged from the bathroom. After flushing and washing her hands, she turned on her camera and scrolled through, looking for *Poker Players.* Meanwhile, Ken caught sight of the canvas of Abe basking in lamplight.

"Holy shit! You did that?" Ken stooped for a better look. "Are you, like, famous?"

"No."

"I can't believe you made that amoeba look good. Lemme see the kids' book."

Marcie grabbed one out of the closet.

Ken flipped through the pages. "I'm impressed."

"You want a soda?" Marcie offered, remembering the correct word for *pop.*

"Nah, I gotta get goin'. If I'm late for this job interview Chrissy set up, I'll be couch surfing for sure or sleeping here on your floor. How come you don't have any furniture?"

"I just got here."

"Yeah. Shipping's slow."

Marcie let Ken believe his conclusion. When the door banged shut behind him, she stared resentfully at the thermostat and tapped it down to eighty-two before showering and changing into shorts. After a late lunch beside the pool, she finished *Saint Abe*, then headed back toward her suite at about the same time Tim entered through the gate on his bicycle, grocery bags dangling from his handlebars. It was not a planned accident this time.

"How was your night in Clearwater?" he asked.

Marcie's mouth dropped. This place was worse than a small town for gossip.

"I ran into Ken getting groceries," Tim said, explaining how he'd come by the knowledge. "Sorry for the way I passed out on you the other night. See what you'd'a been in for? I work, sleep, and see my therapist. And I'm mad most of the time. I used to have a house and a car and I went on expensive vacations. Then I had to sell everything to give her half, even though she married some rich ass from New York. So I have to start all over again from nothing, while she makes a fresh start as a millionairess."

"That'd be hard to take," Marcie agreed.

"An' resentment and regret aren't real good places to start a relationship from. Most of the time, my pills help me not to act out my mood. I thought I might try with you, but I don't got nothin' to offer nobody right now. So don't take it personal."

Marcie tearfully nodded. What else could she do. Once a man's mind was made up, nothing changed it.

Except maybe another woman. She'd never been the one to.

Tim shifted uncomfortably. "'Kay, well, I'm goin' home to make dinner and pass out again in front of the TV, like I do every night. Or maybe pass out before dinner. And I wonder why I can't gain no weight." Tim chuckled, stepped on a pedal, and pushed off to his breezeway.

Tears dribbled down Marcie's cheeks, as she unlocked her door and got hit by an eighty-two-degree cold front. She dumped her sketch stuff, switched the thermostat off, then plunged face down on her mattress to cry. There'd be no Tim. Ever. He'd just—for what now, the third time?—sealed off all hope. Why couldn't she get *no* through her thick, not skull, but heart? Her luck obviously wasn't changing down here. Tim was nothing more than a chemical personality, like Pat had said. Someone she'd be better off without. If he did make a date, she'd wonder if he'd show up for it. Yet she still longed to be with him: the gorgeous, smiling, seemingly happy, apparently carefree, fun guy she experienced the first night, despite the fact he described himself otherwise. She'd even seen that miserable guy he said he was, so when was she going to stop believing in that imaginary potential she always concocted, rather than listening to what a man was telling and showing her, without making stupid excuses, or conveniently forgetting what she did not want to see or know? And then move the hell on, instead of hoping the outcome could still, by some miracle, turn out to be different, meaning the way she wanted.

Maybe things would change now, after meeting Stan. Maybe he'd come along to show her she could like different kinds of men. Men who'd treat her better, or at least show up more than once. Which meant she'd have to meet someone new, because nothing different was going to happen with Tim. Ever. She sniffled herself into more nightmares.

In the morning, red puffy eyes stared back at her from the mirror. Why waste time in paradise being miserable over a man when she was living her dream? Being in the tropics, painting full time, and not working as a waitress should be reasons enough to celebrate every day. And her place had warmed up again. But her heart still ached. She turned the air back on and got on with what she came here to do, which was paint. After breakfast, she walked over to the discount store to print off her Clearwater pictures and buy a shark magazine, along with a blanket and sweats.

The rest of the morning she spent by the pool, paint-mapping a Clearwater Beach montage, with the lifeguard in his tower, watching kids romp in a surf peppered with shark fins. Kind of twisted, but what she felt like doing. Maybe why she wasn't famous: her subject material didn't line up with popular taste. In the afternoon, she sketched out a composite of the Clearwater hotel.

When it got too dark to see, she came in for dinner and noticed a vile bug of a different sort trek across the carpet. This one was smaller, not too big to kill, but before she could grab paper towels, it made its way under the baseboard and vanished.

Marcie waited for it to come out but it didn't. What if those things were like mice—for every one seen, ten more lurked in the walls? They could lay eggs! Get in the food. Crawl into her bed at night, which reminded her of that tickle she felt her second night here under the sheet. She shuddered. Her apartment could be infested! A result of her turning off the AC? And leaving the patio door open? Not that anything so large could stuff its way in through a screen, though some could have got in as babies and, once in, grown up! People would call her a stupid Canadian. Worse, she'd have to live with those things. Now she'd really never sleep.

She scrutinized the baseboards and visually combed the carpet. Not a trace of an insect.

After a while, her stomach reminded her she'd been hungry. She threw a piece of bread in the toaster. While waiting for it to pop, she opened the fridge to see what else she could make, then noticed the same big amber bug on the wall! Not expecting it to have reappeared there, and wound up from keeping vigilance, she involuntarily screamed and ran for a shoe. After whacking the insect a couple times, it fell to the floor, but instead of dying, it kept walking! Sobbing, she hit it again and again, yelling "Die, you motherfucker!" until she heard its shell crunch, and it stopped moving. She unrolled a wad of paper towel, pinched up the carcass, and dropped it into the trash.

"Everything okay in there?" a voice called from the other side of the door.

Marcie stopped. Still shaking, she answered, "Fine. Thanks. Yeah."

Then the toaster popped, launching, along with her toast, another one of those bugs! At which point, she heard herself scream. The bug wasn't even dead. It marched across the counter and dropped onto the floor, where she beat on it with the shoe and screeched, "Die, you sonofabitch!"

"You sure?" The voice again.

Marcie paused, heart pounding. "Fine," she croaked.

"You don't sound fine."

She wasn't.

"Would you like me to call anyone? Or come in?"

"Yes," she acceded. She could use somebody to talk to. But that meant a stranger—a neighbour, likely—would see her unglued, though at this point, she didn't much care. The same instant the door swung open on its hinges, she flung herself at the man on the other side.

"I'm glad I came by." He chuckled, squeezing her in a hug. "I was just leaving Jim's and heard you screaming bloody murder and hittin' something, so I thought I'd check."

"There's these bugs, they're huge and have wings. The other one the other day was like this big black butterfly but these ones were amber coloured. They were crawling across the carpet and up the wall. One came out of the toaster without being dead, and there's one under the baseboards that's still in there now!" She sobbed out the whole story.

He laughed. "You got cockroaches!"

Marcie stiffened. Cockroaches? Those were something filthy people had. She wasn't filthy. So how could she have cockroaches?

"Nothin' t'be ashamed of," he consoled, as if reading her horror. "Everybody in Florida's got 'em." He loosened his hug. "You want me to come in?"

"Yes." Marcie opened the door, grateful not to have to be alone, even if the man looked like a gangster, though just because he dressed in those baggy shorts that hung past the knee and were belted up somewhere mid-ass under an extra-large T-shirt, and wore his baseball cap backwards, didn't mean he was one. A lot of guys here dressed like that, and he'd just come from Jim's, which made him a friend of a friend. Besides, what'd she have in here to steal?

"Or maybe we could go for a walk," she suggested. Because she didn't really want to stay inside with cockroaches. Plus, she was hungry. And didn't want to eat anything now that hadn't been in the fridge, a place—hopefully—where those bugs couldn't get in, but if they could, they likely wouldn't die in there either, because if extreme heat didn't kill them, cold might not either.

He chuckled. "I don't think you want to do that."

"Why? It's a nice night. Why doesn't anybody here want to be outside at night?"

He raised his eyebrows as if a five-year-old would know the answer to that and nodded toward the end of the breezeway which didn't exit onto the parking lot, but the courtyard, signalling her to go check something out for herself.

Curious, Marcie walked out into the heavily vegetated common area. As soon as her feet touched the grass, dozens of bugs the size of small birds dove at her. Sobbing, she ran back to the man.

"That's why." He smirked, wiping at a tear with his thumb. "Hey. I saw your paintin' of our poker game while I was droppin' off Abe."

Our? Dropping off Abe? Which made this man, *That little weasel,* in Chrissy's words? The one who'd run off after accusing his fellow players of cheating?

He gently picked a bug out of her hair and flicked it into the night. Which sent Marcie into a fresh spasm of hysteria. "Are those all cockroaches too?"

"Yup. Though pretty soon, it'll be too cold for 'em. Meanwhile, if I was you, I'd call the office to have your place fumigated. You shouldn'ta left your patio door open like you been doin'."

He'd known who she was and where she lived all along. "The porch is screened in," Marcie feebly argued.

"Aw, honey, on the ground floor, they crawl in under the railing."

"Oh," Of course. If they could squeeze under baseboards, a wood beam abutting cement wouldn't pose much of a barrier.

He stroked her hair. "Hey, you wanna chill at my place for a while? I ain't got no roaches. I'm on the third floor and I know to keep my windows shut. Bring your camera. You can do a painting of me." He pulled a roll of cash out of his baggy shorts' pocket and peeled off a bill. "As a down payment."

What did men here have against wallets? "One hundred dollars."

"Go on. Take it. Jim said you're tryin' t' make your livin' as an artist. So I'm offerin' work."

Marcie accepted the money.

"'Kay. Go get what you need and lock up." He wandered in and studied her painting of Abe. "You are good," he called loud enough to be heard through the closed bathroom door. "Look at that motherfucker. You almost made him seem holy. All you left out's the halo."

Marcie emerged from the bathroom as the guy took a piece of gum out of his mouth.

"Where's your trash?"

"Under the sink."

He opened the cupboard door and then moaned.

"What?"

"Aw, baby girl! You can't leave them things in there like that."

Marcie came to see what he was looking at. Her trash bag writhed with ants! She scuttled back several feet as she screamed.

The man grabbed a fresh garbage bag and dumped the one with the ants into it, then sprayed the escaped and remaining ants, along with the whole area, with the spay cleaner, wiped everything up, put the towels in the bag, tied it up, then headed outside, presumably to the dumpster—just as Tim walked past. Of all the stupid luck! Why was he awake and outside? Had he mixed up his pills? He'd see this guy leaving her breezeway with a garbage bag in his hand. Jim's breezeway also, yes, but why would one man be taking out another man's trash, and so late at night? So Tim would conclude whose bag it was. And also that she was probably sleeping with this guy, or why else would he be taking out her trash? With any luck, Tim might be too busy brooding over his own recovery problems to be paying much attention to one of Jim's friends or where he'd emerged from or what he carried. Yeah, right. Though, why should she care what Tim concluded? It wasn't like being with another man would ruin her chances of having Tim. He'd made it very plain that they wouldn't be getting together. So why shouldn't she move on? Hadn't he said himself she should find someone better? Though how much better was a man whose friends accused him of being a thief? Still, she couldn't help but care what Tim thought. Which meant what? She wanted him to believe she was pining for him, so he'd realize how much he meant to her and come running? Dumb, she knew. She just didn't want him thinking she was a slut; first, staying over in Clearwater, and now this, a cheater taking her trash out.

Maybe she only thought what Tim would think and he wasn't thinking at all, beyond subtracting his bank balance from the price of a down payment for a house to calculate how much more he needed to save. Or maybe contemplating taking a new pill purported to keep a man's dick harder longer—in the States, pharmaceutical companies were allowed to advertise on TV—to compensate for how his current pills had impacted his performance, so maybe seeing—she didn't even know the Hispanic man's name, whom she was practically on her way home with—a man carrying a bag of trash wouldn't trigger Tim to think of Marcie at all. But the Hispanic guy wasn't just a man to Tim; they'd played poker together, which made them acquaintances, which would mean an exchange of polite dialogue, like, *Hey, how's it going?* Or, *Wazz up?* Leading to a reply of, *You meet the new Canadian?* Which would draw an affirmative, *Yeah,* from Tim. To which her new friend would respond, *She's all freaked about cockroaches, bless the Lord, so I'm just takin' her home to offer her comfort.* Tim's expression might then cloud with disgust, while he'd be forced to utter some congratulatory comment to a fellow male for scoring.

When the man returned, he was grinning. "Tonight, I have come to appreciate cockroaches like never before." He put his arm around her and guided her toward a rusty junk heap of a car, yet when he turned the key in the ignition, the engine rumbled like a finely tuned racing machine. Not a sound she expected. Also surprising, the stereo whoomped in state-of-the-art surround sound, not tinny radio, which would seem more in line with the car.

"You like reggaeton?" The man turned up the music. "Chrissy probably told you some nasty things about me, but judge for yourself 'steada listenin' t' gossip."

"She did say something about you, but she didn't mention your name."

"Emilio."

"Marcie."

"I know." He kissed her, then turned the car in the direction of the gate instead of the ring road. Was he kidnapping her?

"I thought you said you lived on the other side of the property." Though if he did, why hadn't she heard his car before? *Oh, right.* Because she'd been keeping her windows closed. Windows designed to withstand hurricanes must be pretty soundproof.

"I just gotta do one errand first. I thought you might like to come with me."

While the car gate opened, Tim entered the pedestrian gate. Marcie bent down to scratch her ankle, though Tim had probably already seen her, or had been informed of their togetherness, and Emilio might now think she didn't want to be seen with him. Which wouldn't bode well.

Once the gate finished opening, Emilio drove through it, turned down the lane and onto the highway, after checking for on-coming traffic—unlike Chrissy. At least in one respect, she'd feel safe.

"Tim's work."

"What is?"

"The engine. As a down payment for a favour he chickened outta having done in New York. He was supposed to do the exterior once the matter was taken care of, but I think the car's better this way. It attracts less attention."

From deaf people?

After a few miles, he asked if she wanted a soda or anything.

"If you're getting one."

He pulled into a convenience store and parked in front of the gas pump closest to the door and left the engine running. He told her to wait in the car, darted in, then trotted out with two cans. After quickly settling himself behind the wheel, he passed her a can and stuffed the other between his legs.

"Thanks." Marcie snapped the tab.

He drove on for a bit, then said out of nowhere, "I can't wait to break you off."

Marcie went cold. Her legs turned to jelly. "Why?" she whispered in panic. As punishment for hiding from Tim?

"Why?" he questioned her question. "You're gorgeous. And all that fire inside you? The way you was beatin' them motherfuckers. Damn! I bet you're a wild one in bed!"

"In bed?"

"What's wrong? You're not frigid or something, are you?"

"Frigid?"

"Yeah. Like, you got issues with sex?"

"Sex?"

"Like somebody rape you or something?"

"No."

"Then? Why you sittin' there like you seen a ghost? Is there a problem I should know about?"

"No. Sex? That's what that means?"

"What's what mean?"

"Break you off."

Emilio roared. "Aw, baby girl! Ain't you never heard that expression before?"

Marcie shook her head.

"What'd you think I meant?"

Some kind of chainsaw murder was nothing she wanted to admit to thinking. He didn't seem to be the type who'd overlook such an insult. "I don't know."

"So you're good? With having sex?"

"Yes. Normal sex," she clarified. Meaning nothing too kinky from which she could accidentally die.

He laughed, shook his head, and rubbed his hand on her leg. "I don't mean just sex, either. I want to get to know you. As a person."

Which seemed even more shocking. Emilio, a rumoured no-good, wanted to explore a relationship?

After about fifteen more minutes of speedy threading through traffic, Emilio turned off onto a side street, then another one, and pulled into a driveway. "I'll just be a minute." He leaned across the seat and kissed her, slammed his door, bopped around to the trunk, collected a small package, walked up the front walk—probably getting dive-bombed by cockroaches—rang the bell, passed off the package, took some cash, stuffed it in his pocket, and returned to the car.

So Emilio dealt drugs. Hopefully all Chrissy meant by "no good." Drug dealers didn't usually go around killing people. They made too much money.

"Okay, all done. You want to go eat or go home?"

Home. Like they shared one. Could she see herself married to him? If she needed him to do her a favour so she could stay in the States? "Home's good."

Emilio drove back to Palm Grove and parked in a space on the far side of the grounds near Ken and Chrissy's; she recognized Chrissy's car.

Emilio opened the door to a stark living room, which reflected nothing of his personality. The furniture—a combination of steel, white leather, and glass—gleamed spotless. She would have expected something more lived-in, like a beat-up couch draped with blankets, some rattan chairs, wobbly wood tables, dust, and maybe some candles stuck into empty wine bottles.

"You need to use the bathroom?"

"Yeah." Once she closed the door, she peeked in the medicine cabinet. No pills. No women's cosmetics, though would he be bringing her to his place if he shared it with a wife or common-law girlfriend? Just one toothbrush, toothpaste, mouthwash, nail clippers, and shaving stuff. And, okay, one bottle of generic pain killers; everybody kept those for the odd headache. Marcie turned on the shower.

Emilio stuck his head in the door. "Mind if I join you?"

After rinsing off the day's sweat and stress, they crawled under a down-filled duvet! Why didn't people just turn down the AC And save money? Especially now that she knew cockroaches didn't spontaneously generate from warm air. But, there was mold to think about, Ken had said. Still, the temperature in Emilio's apartment had to be at least ten degrees cooler than the lease-mandated eighty degrees.

In the morning, after a lot of good sex and a nightmare-less sleep snuggled into Emilio, she woke to the touch of his hand caressing her hip.

After more sex, he declared, "I want to take you out and show you off."

Out? In daylight? Was she still dreaming?

He slapped her ass in an up-and-at-'em kind of way. "Why don't you go home and dress up and we'll go someplace fancy for brunch."

This *was* serious. But, "I don't have any dress clothes."

"Go buy something." He reached into his pocket and peeled a couple hundreds off his cash roll. "You drive?"

"Yeah."

He tossed her his car keys. "I'll be at Jim's."

Stunned at a man giving her money instead of asking to borrow some, *and* letting her drive his car, when most men didn't even want her *in* theirs for fear of her shedding a telltale hair their wives or girlfriends would find, Marcie stuck the bills in her purse and walked down the stairs. Life really had turned around.

After reverently starting the engine, power thrummed up her arms. What if Tim looked out the window and saw her drive past in Emilio's car? She reminded herself that he would have likely heard Emilio's car go by enough times that he wouldn't even glance out the window. She backed out of the parking space and cruised the ring road. While waiting for the gate to open, she shut off the AC.

After checking for traffic at the end of the lane, she pulled onto the highway and stomped on the gas to test the acceleration. In a flood of dizzy adrenalin, she let herself blast past the turn-off to the mall and kept going until she got stuck behind traffic, then pulled a U-ie, like everybody else did down here, to turn around and go back. Wow.

The typical freezing blast of cold air hit her as soon as she opened the mall doors. The mannequins were at least dressed for the low temperatures, sporting wool skirts and sweaters, and even heavy jackets, hats, mitts, and boots! Chrissy had mentioned winter was coming, but all that winter wear seemed like overkill. Equally as weird, stores were decorated for Halloween. Monsters, goblins, witches, and jack-o-lanterns just didn't go with summer heat and palm trees. Spooky creatures accompanied dead leaves and nippy air.

After rooting through a clearance sale, she found a lacy white summer dress, and in another store, some white sandals.

"Very sexy," Emilio approved, giving her the once-over when he opened Jim's door after she knocked.

She waved hi to Jim as she passed Emilio his change, which he took, and his keys, which he didn't. "You drive."

He directed her onto the interstate and told her to open it up. Marcie wove her way into the left lane and did. Like she'd done on her way to the mall.

"Not bad!" Emilio praised. "I'm gonna haff t'get you to replace Abe. Slow it down over the bridge."

After crossing it, he directed her into a convenience store/gas station.

"Stop here . . ."

Which was just past the front door, not in a parking space. Again.

". . . and leave it running."

What was he going to do, rob the store? A joke-thought, which too quickly turned into what could be a real possibility. But in a pink suit? A little conspicuous, and drug dealers usually weren't thieves; she'd known enough of them in Calgary. They made too much cash selling drugs to risk being busted for relative chump change. Maybe that was what he was doing. Another drug deal. But he hadn't brought in a package, like he had to the house last night. Though how much room did a few grams of narcotics take up? His baggy pants' pockets could accommodate and conceal several kilos. Fashion with function.

But, if Emilio was in there delivering, that would make her an accomplice. Lovely. Fast track back to Canada—if the cops didn't shoot them first in a car chase or throw them in an American jail. Continuing a relationship with a drug dealer wouldn't be smart if she wanted to stay in the States.

The longer he remained gone, the more her palms sweated. She turned the AC back on and, not thinking that her sweaty hands might have picked up dirt from the wheel, wiped them on her new dress, leaving black smears.

Smart. Actually, a little grime might be a good thing. It'd make her an *embarrassment.* Then Emilio would stop taking her places. And if she wasn't out in public doing things with him, or with him while he was doing things, she'd be less likely to get arrested. Ironic. Usually she complained about not going on dates; now, on a date, she'd suddenly come to wish she wasn't on one.

What was taking him? He'd been in there forever. Had something gone wrong? Maybe an undercover cop was inside buying coffee and Emilio had to wait for him to leave? Or he was robbing the store and the clerk had pulled out a gun? Or maybe Emilio had run into a friend. Or had become friends with someone who worked there and was just shooting the shit. She'd had regular customers she talked to at work. And some who liked talking to her more than she liked talking to them. Maybe that was why Emilio had left her in the car, as an excuse to escape. *Well, gotta go; my girlfriend's outside with the car running.* Stopped where the licence plate couldn't be seen from inside.

The store door finally opened and Emilio burst out at the same high-wired speed he always moved at. As soon as he got in the car, before he even had the door closed, she'd shifted into gear and taken off, but without squealing the tires. If he'd done anything illegal, she didn't want to be attracting unnecessary attention, nor hanging around to get caught.

"Whoa." But he didn't mean stop. He grinned, pleased. "That's my girl." And buckled his seatbelt, tightening his pants over a bulge, though a little too far to the right to be what sometimes bulged in men's pants. After checking her position in traffic, she glanced down again at the lump not quite in his crotch, but he'd put his hand in his pocket. To shift the lump, or to be ready to pull something out, like a gun? A thought which made Marcie further stiffen. Was he expecting a car chase? Marcie swallowed. Maybe he planned on holding her hostage if they didn't escape apprehension. She gripped the wheel tighter.

"'Kay. Take the next exit west," Emilio instructed.

Marcie checked the rearview before changing lanes.

"What's wrong?" he demanded.

"I always shoulder check."

"That's not what I meant. You got a death grip on the steering wheel all of a sudden. Your knuckles are white."

"Pale Canadian." Marcie chuckled.

"Bullshit. You're out baking in the sun every day. You're browner than I am. Relax."

Marcie loosened her grip.

"It's not this, is it?" He pulled a gun out of his pocket and practically aimed it at her.

He wouldn't shoot her while she was driving, would he? He didn't seem suicidal, though murder-suicides weren't that unheard of. But usually men offed longer-time girlfriends and had a better reason to and did the shooting at home, not on the road. Had Jim said something to Emilio about her being hot for Tim? Or worse, did she talk in her sleep? Had she accidentally moaned Tim's name while they were having sex? Otherwise, Emilio should have no reason to shoot or kidnap her. She had relatively no money, which he should have figured out if she didn't even own a nice dress or have any furniture; her net wealth had been pre-sunk into rent. No one she knew had money, and he wouldn't know who she knew up in Canada, anyway, and everyone here lived pay cheque to pay cheque. But . . . if he killed for fun, he'd picked a good target. Who'd miss her if she disappeared? If anyone asked where she'd gone, Emilio could shrug and say back to Canada. Not a comforting thought, though he shouldn't need a gun to kill a woman forty pounds lighter than himself. He could choke her with his bare hands. Then toss her body to the sharks to get rid of it. Maybe he packed a piece simply because the American constitution allowed him his God-given right to bear arms.

"No," Marcie croaked. "Okay, yes," she confessed. "It is that. I'm Canadian. We're not used to guns."

Emilio shook his head, probably at all the things she wasn't used to. And she wasn't. She felt like she'd moved to a new country. Which she had. But she'd expected it to be more the same.

"What are you going to do with it?" Marcie couldn't help voicing.

"In my line of work, I just like havin' it. In case I run into trouble."

"What *do* you do?" Marcie ventured another personal question. Something which someone who was sleeping with someone should know. Yet in his case, felt like an overly invasive and personal question. "Since we're"— What were they, after one night?—"getting to know each other, it'd be weird not to know." She justified her question.

"I sell lingerie."

"Lingerie?"

"Hand-stitched in Puerto Rico."

"Really?"

"What'd you think I did?"

Marcie shrugged. "Not that."

"You assumed I was selling drugs, didn't you?"

"That package last night . . ."

"Bras."

"Bras?"

"Summa these guys are cross-dressers and wanna keep it discreet. Like the guy in the convenience store today. Or they want to surprise their little lady."

"Oh." And that required a gun why?

"When we get to where we're going, I'll show you. Take the next exit." He further directed her to a quaint, village-like, downtown area in St. Petersburg with salmon-coloured, Spanish-style buildings, and quaint brick streets. He had her park in a lot with thatched roof canopies over the stalls to protect the cars from the sun. Then got out and opened the trunk.

Sure enough, inside were boxes of feather boas, glittery costumes, G-strings, crotchless panties, regular bras in all sizes, garters, stockings, negligees, corsets, masks, camisoles, teddies, and transparent skirts.

"I also sell to strippers and their clients. Which is why I like havin' the gun. Those places can get pretty rough. You like this?" He held up a lacy camisole, then slipped it into her purse. "Let's go."

He took her hand and led her along a path to a mammoth brick plantation-style mansion. A giant front porch converted into a restaurant patio jutted over the water. This place sure as hell didn't remind her of any place she'd worked at, or even been to before.

"What happened to your dress?" Emilio noticed on their way up the stone walk.

"Oh. I just wiped my hands. I didn't realize . . ."

Emilio shook his head and put his hand on her lower back, leading her in the glass door, undeterred. She wished she could be here with Tim, or, spectacular as this place was, even snuggled up with him on his couch, watching TV, in his air-conditioned living room with the drapes pulled.

Once inside, Emilio put his arm around her and she put her arm around him, careful not to let her hand touch the gun in his pocket, as if not touching the lethal weapon would make it go away. It didn't create a bulge when he stood.

On their walk through the tiled lobby—finally a place with no carpet—on their way to the dining room, he switched the gun to his other pocket and pulled her closer. Couldn't he have just had her switch sides? Or had he wanted an excuse to wave his gun around? No one appeared to notice. Were people oblivious? Or was it that a gun wasn't anything out of the ordinary, south of the border, even in classy places? The patrons even ignored his pink suit. Safer, likely, making a show of minding their own business than openly paying heed to a possibly known gangster.

Maybe, at that very moment, some discreet concierge was calling the cops. If he wasn't, that said something, too. How many rules had she bent, and seen bent, for regular customers? Or maybe the staff was simply preoccupied with their own tasks, or hung over, or still high or half drunk.

Emilio requested a table for two. "On the patio if you have something."

An unnecessary tag. No one sat on patios in the day, either, yet the inside tables were packed.

Calypso music bonged softly inside and out, just like at Gilligan's in Clearwater, as the maître d' led them outside. Even the patio tables were elegant, set with the same pastel-green cloths. She should be charmed. And she was overwhelmed that a man had taken her here, and had even bought her a dress, but part of her wondered what the hell she was doing. Cockroaches didn't seem quite as bad in the morning, or compared to what she could be getting into by becoming involved with Emilio. Usually, not something she'd ever had to worry about; *getting involved* with a man.

The cement floor glared white, especially outside the shadow of the awning. Pink antique crystal wine goblets refracted the sunlight, casting random rainbows. Silver flatware gleamed in the brightness. Properly placed to the left of the forks, lilac bread-and-butter plates served as nests for yellow napkin birds. In the middle of every table towered a slender mother-of-pearl vase containing a white rose. The view of the mansions across the water added the crowning touch of decadence.

When the waiter came, Emilio ordered amaretto and orange juice for both of them. "Doubles. You'll like those."

"I do."

"I bet you've never had one with Florida fresh-squeezed."

"I haven't. And I've never been anywhere so incredible." She reached in her purse for her camera. Emilio smiled in a pose. She shot him and just about everything else. But still he remained unembarrassed. Then she thought of her tubal! That would dissuade him from sticking around. Hispanics were big on big families. She'd let him know she didn't want—and couldn't have—kids. That should bring a no-fault end to their dating and send him searching for somebody else. But how to bring up the topic?

Their drinks came.

"Cheers," Emilio toasted. "To us."

Marcie gently clinked her glass to his and sipped. "Mmmm." The alcohol went straight to her head and sparked an idea. "I bet this is the kind of place you'd like to bring your kids to one day."

"Maybe one day. But right now, they're a little young for formal dining."

A response Marcie hadn't expected. "You have kids already?"

"I know I don't look it, but I'm thirty-six."

"Oh."

Emilio looked at her weirdly. "If you didn't know I had kids, why'd you say, *your kids*?"

"I meant the hypothetical kids you might want to have someday. To see if you wanted any. Most men do, but I don't. I just wanted you to know that. Right off the bat. That I'm not having kids. My tubes are tied. So you wouldn't think that someday I'd be having yours and blame me 'cause I didn't say something sooner." Now she'd have to come up with another ruse.

"That's good, because I have three girls already. I love 'em to death, but I don't want any more or a woman who wants any. So that makes you more perfect."

Lovely. But his story didn't add up. She hadn't seen any kids' stuff in his apartment. Like toys. Even if they lived with their mother, wouldn't they keep something of theirs at their dad's? "Don't they visit?"

"I live with 'em."

"But I didn't see any kids' stuff."

"Actually, that's Joe's place I took you to."

"Who's Joe?"

"My partner."

One more sip of that drink, and Marcie might have blurted out, *You're bisexual?*

"Business partner," he clarified.

98

"Oh." Marcie nodded. So, Joe made the lingerie? And spent most of his time in Puerto Rico? Instinct told her not to ask.

"I'll introduce you when he gets out."

Out? Of jail? The military? Rehab? The hospital? Puerto Rico?

"How old are your kids?" she asked instead.

"Five, seven, and nine."

Too young to stay on their own, and nine wasn't old enough to babysit. So, "Who's with them now?"

"Their mother."

"Oh."

"She looks after 'em when I work, and I have to be there when she's at work. So I'm glad this came up too. So you'll understand why I can't spend every night with you. Penny's a nurse."

And so would have to take night shifts at the hospital.

"But I can pop in every morning and afternoon when I come by to get Abe or drop him off, 'cause then the kids are in school."

"So you still live with your wife," Marcie clarified.

"Technically . . ." he hedged. "But it's not a real marriage."

"Oh." Which gave her another out. "Well, to be honest, I'm kind of looking to find somebody to marry, so I can stay in the States."

"No problem. Joe'll marry you. All the women like him and he'll get extra points with his parole officer if he's hitched."

Which explained where Joe was, but that was also a reason not to marry him. Because, how would Immigration take her being married to a criminal, or rather, an ex-con? "I'm guessing Joe doesn't have kids?" she sought to establish, hoping he did. "Because I don't want to be a stepmother either."

"Not that he knows about." Emilio winked. "Joe's not really the father type. He owns a strip club."

Hence the partnership. Joe probably forced his strippers to buy their costumes from Emilio. And in return, Emilio did what for Joe? All this made her uneasy.

Their waiter arrived to take their order.

"What are you having?" Emilio opened his menu.

"Maybe a fruit salad."

"That's it? You haven't eaten since yesterday. Unless you grabbed something at the mall." Emilio looked up at the waiter. "Give us a minute." When he left, he said, "Okay, what gives?" Emilio crossed his arms on the table and leaned forward.

"I haven't met Joe."

"You will."

"So I can decide then? Because I'm not making any commitments before . . ."

"Of course not. I'm not forcing you. It was just an idea the two of you can discuss."

"Okay. Good. Because I just don't want you thinking it's a done deal."

"No. I just don't want to lose my baby girl to Canada."

"Joe wouldn't care that . . . You mean, you and I would still be . . ."

"Hell, no, he wouldn't care."

"When's Joe getting out?"

"November."

Another month and a bit.

"Are you ready to order a decent meal now?"

"Yeah."

"You don't look ready. Something's still bothering you."

"Okay. It's the gun," Marcie spilled. "I'm Canadian. We're not used to guns. Nobody I've ever been with has carried one. Being with you makes me nervous. When I know you have one."

Emilio narrowed his eyes. "How many's that?"

"How many's what?"

"How many men have you been with?"

Fear flooded Marcie, as it had so often since meeting Emilio. How many men would he think was too many?

"Approximately," Emilio prodded. "Ten? Twenty?"

A conservative estimate for one year during most of her twenties. Add up a decade of taking someone home from the bar damn near every weekend . . . though things had slowed down the last couple of years. "Twenty," Marcie settled on, which Emilio obviously thought a high number. "I've never been seen as long-term material. Men in Calgary don't stay with anybody who doesn't want to have kids or pay half a mortgage. And I was never into half-owning a house. What about you?" Because he didn't exactly come off as a man who'd had few partners, either. "How many women have you slept with?"

"You're the fifth."

Oh, come on. She almost laughed.

"I guess that's a part of you I'll have to overlook. So, you ready to order?" Emilio signalled the waiter.

"Do you have French toast?" Marcie asked the waiter, which should be substantial enough, and she wouldn't have to finish it—unless he put his gun to her head, unlikely in public.

"That's better," Emilio approved, as if praising a three-year-old. He ordered bacon and eggs over hard.

"Another round?" the waiter offered.

"Maybe just a plain orange juice," Marcie insisted.

"Same," Emilio said.

Their meals arrived soon after, heavily garnished with fluff that cost less than a dollar and probably added about fifteen to the price.

When the bill came, Emilio paid with a hundred. Then he said he had a surprise. Like there hadn't been enough of those already. He led her by the hand along some water, then pointed to a sign partially hidden by palm trees. "The Salvador Dali museum!" Marcie practically squealed. "I love Dali's work!"

"I thought you would. Yours reminds me a bit of his."

He paid their way in with another hundred, even though he had smaller bills.

After gawking at six-foot-tall, intricately painted canvases of religious battle scenes, skeletons riding bicycles around a grand piano, a baby's face with a map on it, a cracked globe with a muscular person struggling out, and other paintings she'd seen in art books—all of them stunning her speechless—Emilio said he'd buy her whatever she liked from the gift shop. She chose a relatively inexpensive book showing his complete works. He used another hundred to pay.

"Okay, let's go. I gotta be back. Penny's nights start tonight."

Good, because after seeing Dali, Marcie wanted to paint.

Emilio let her out outside the gate. "Here." He handed her a key. "Stay at Joe's till your place gets fumigated." Then he kissed her goodbye.

Pat stood at her door, holding two cans of beer.

"That was a long date."

How did he . . .?

"I heard you guys leave this morning. I live next to Joe's," Pat explained. "Did that little shit tell you that isn't his place?"

"Yeah," Marcie nodded.

"And that he's married?"

"That too."

"And you're still seein' him?"

Marcie shrugged, shook her head, and nodded all at the same time.

"What the hell were you doing?" Pat stared at the stains on her dress.

"We went out for lunch."

"He pay with a hundred?"

"Yeah."

"Looks like a little of that ink rubbed off on your dress."

"Ink?"

"Don't tell him I said anything. I don't want to get shot. Anyway, I heard him drop you off and came out to see if you wanted to come to a pool tournament."

"Now?"

"In a couple of minutes. We're just waiting for the cab." He handed her a beer.

"I drank enough today," Marcie declined.

"Does Emilio know he's your second choice?"

"No. And don't tell him. I don't want to get shot either."

"He give you this?" Pat plucked the camisole out of her purse by the strap that'd been hanging out.

"Yeah."

"At least it doesn't have padded cups." He tossed it back in.

Abe emerged on scene.

"Better be careful," Pat warned him, "or Marcie's gonna put you out of a job."

Abe didn't look worried, but then he didn't seem like the type to concern himself with much of anything. "He take you flimflammin'?"

"What's that?"

But Ken approached before either Pat or Abe could answer, swinging a leather case containing, likely, a pool cue. "Is the cab here?"

"Does it look like it?" Pat asked back. Then checked, "So. Are you coming?"

"I kind of want to paint." Marcie hesitated. "I've been out all day."

"You can paint all day tomorrow. And the day after that. This tournament's a big deal. Thousand bucks first prize." Pat tried to persuade her. "Should be exciting."

"Yeah?" She was no tournament player herself, but in the bar, while waiting to go on shift, she'd played with enough tournament players coming in to practice. And where else was there to go after work at three in the morning besides pool halls, where guys fell over each other to give her pointers in hopes of taking her home? Sometimes, she went with them. "How much is the entry fee?"

"Register if you want, but don't get your hopes up 'cause I always win," Ken warned her.

Ken looked too drunk to play.

"Cab's here." He pointed. "You guys comin' or not?"

Why not? The evening could earn her another whole month to paint.

"Okay, nobody fart!" Ken grinned.

The bar looked like a set from a 1950s honky-tonk movie, with cracked leather booths, warped hardwood floors, peanut shells, smoky air, cartoon paintings of buxom women in bikinis, and neon signs advertising beer brands. TVs hanging from the ceiling posed the only modern intrusion. A wrinkled woman with a ponytail who probably used to be cute poured and served drinks. *Like looking in the mirror.* Marcie shivered. Herself in another twenty years if she'd stayed in the business. At the far end of the room stood the pool tables, each presided over by a classic low-hanging stained-glass dome lamp.

She followed Ken to the sign-in table and asked the organizers if they took last-minute entries.

"Seriously?" Ken questioned. "You think you can play at this level?"

"One way to find out." Marcie smiled and took out a bill. Ken snooped at it.

"Better not use any of Emilio's homemade hundreds here. They have one of those lights to check."

Which confirmed Pat's earlier allusion to ink. Marcie had hundreds. Three from Jim, which could have come from Abe as rent, passing on his pay from Emilio. The ones she spent at the mall? She could have been busted there. Or they both could have been arrested at the restaurant. *Shit.*

Marcie took her number and headed to her designated table and rolled all the nineteen-ounce cues on it. No point thinking what could have happened now. Just focus on winning one thousand legitimate dollars and hope her relationship history would repeat itself again, meaning Emilio would leave, though this time, she doubted he would. Why did her luck have to change now? She chose the least warped cue and put the rest back. Everybody else had brought his own, and yes, *his*, because she was the only girl playing. To warm up, she leaned over the table and slid the shaft of her selection back and forth on the bridge of flesh between her thumb and first knuckle.

"You're playing?" Chrissy materialized. "Ken always wins the thousand bucks."

"I heard."

"Oh, and thanks for making me look like a *shit,* letting you out on the Veterans Expressway. Ken hasn't stopped goin' on about it."

"You want a drink?" Jim saved Marcie from answering.

"Maybe a soda. Soda *water,*" she qualified, before Jim could ask what kind, or come back with a cola, full of caffeine and sugar. She didn't want her hands shaking or her heart beating any faster than it already was after hearing of Emilio's counterfeiting business. "Mineral water if they don't have it."

Just as Jim returned with a little green bottle, Emilio walked in, this time wearing white shorts and an untucked white silk button-down shirt. And three fat gold chains. "Baby girl! Whachu doin' here? I thought you said you wanted to paint." He hugged her.

"I thought you had to look after your kids."

"I left 'em with a friend."

"They're probably in the car," Chrissy muttered, likely not wanting to be shot, either, for talking too loud. "Every year, he thinks he's gonna take home Ken's money, but this is one game Ken can play."

Emilio bobbed off to pay his entry fee and joined the group to listen as the official read off the rules and explained the rotation.

After shaking hands with her first opponent, Marcie focused on the balls, not on the person or anything else, like trying to see how the others might be playing. She called tails on the toss, winning choice of break, took her option of breaking, then focused on slowing her breathing. One low ball dropped. To follow up, she picked off two more solids hovering near the rims of other pockets, calling each shot, but missed her fourth. Her opponent sank one of hers by accident and swore. Marcie put down the rest of hers, but missed the eight, typically choking under pressure. At least she should have another chance to win before this guy sank his balls, all but one still on the felt. *No pressure*, she chanted, when her turn came again. She pretended the ball was blue to hopefully fool her adrenals into believing this shot wasn't any big deal, so maybe she wouldn't freak out as much, pointed to the side pocket, took aim, and shot. The damn thing plunked in. She tried not to gape in shock but smile as if she expected it.

With the choke-on-the-eight spell broken, she just as easily sank the eight in the next round with a new opponent. No best two out of three in this tournament— one win and move on.

With confidence, she advanced to the third game and won that. Then found herself facing Emilio.

"What?" he asked, as if she'd come to ask him a question.

"Heads or tails?"

"You're playin' me?"

He seemed not to know whether to look proud or horrified. She raised her eyebrows and smiled.

"Shee-it!" He grinned and shook his head. "You know I can't let you win."

"I wouldn't want you to."

"Promise, no hard feelings. I'm here to take that money from Ken."

"Sure." Marcie nodded agreeably.

But Emilio looked a little concerned.

"You can break first if you want," Marcie offered.

He took her up on it, but must have been feeling an uneasy pressure, because he didn't sink anything. Worse for him, a high ball sat in front of every pocket. He practically threw his cue, recognizing even a novice could half run the table on that kind of leave. Which Marcie did.

"Sorry," she apologized insincerely, as she kept picking off balls.

"You didn't tell me you played pool!"

"It didn't come up. And I didn't know about the tournament till I got home."

Too agitated to focus, Emilio missed his next shot and cursed. Pat and Jim cheered.

"Fifteen in the end," Marcie called, with more confidence than she felt. Long shots weren't her forte, but no other options presented themselves. Aiming as far left on the cue ball as possible without risking a scratch, she firmly tapped the tip of the cue at the target spot, sending it on a crisp mission across the table and into the fifteen, which sent it on its anticipated best-case trajectory into the end pocket.

"Son of a bitch!" Emilio swore.

Ecstatic, she maintained a stoic exterior as if she never doubted the outcome, and lined up for the eight. Again, she pictured it being blue; the tactic worked last time. No reason to worry. She'd sunk several eights already tonight. The pattern had broken. She re-chalked her cue, sipped her mineral water, and mentally programmed the ball's path. "Side," she called, before applying what she hoped was the right amount of force instead of getting over-excited and whacking too hard, like she used to do, causing a ricochet. But had she applied enough oomph? Still holding her breath and her follow-through position, she watched the ball creep across the table. *Go, go, go!* She willed it not to run out of momentum. *Click!* Down. Relief.

"Beat by my girl." Emilio shook his head, and, in a forced show of sportsmanship, hugged her. If she was lucky, they'd break up over this. "'Kay, now go kick Ken's ass." Emilio patted hers, converting his opponent into his champion.

Marcie had just enough time to use the bathroom while the outcome of Ken's game still hung in the balance.

"*Motherfuckingsonofabitch!*" exclaimed Ken, when she approached the table they were to play on.

This time, the official tossed the coin.

"Tails," Ken called before it landed.

Tails it was.

"I'll break," Ken claimed his right.

He sunk one low ball, but missed his second shot by a millimeter. Not a mistake an unbeatable player should have made, and, sober, he probably wouldn't have. Or if he'd been less agitated. "I assume the table's open?" Marcie checked with the judge, just in case Americans had different rules, because there were different versions in Canada.

The judge nodded, so Marcie chose another low ball, since one of them was already down and another conveniently left in front of a pocket. She slammed in the solid green with a backspin, which returned the cue ball to her by fortunate accident. It perfectly lined itself up for the fourteen in the end. She followed that success with a long bank—which she confidently called with the same bravado that worked so well last time—and lucked out again. Any uncertainty in her voice and Ken would have screamed, "Fluke!" Instead, he sucked up the rest of his drink while watching her pocket another shot. *Excellent.* A demoralized, angry opponent with even more alcohol in him. She missed her next. So did Ken, applying too much force, causing the thirteen to rapidly ricochet between the edges of the pocket. Another amateur error. Marcie tapped in her last solid with just enough bottom spin to set herself up for the *blue eight.* Emilio danced deliriously on the sidelines.

Ken slammed his drink onto the table, assuming she'd bag the shot. She'd have to now. Summoning an attitude of boredom, she stepped into position. Aim, contact, follow through, watch, *click.*

"*Fuck!*" In a temper, Ken javelined the rubber end of his custom-made cue into the floor.

"Way to go!" Pat congratulated her above the noise of the clapping and cheering. Emilio grabbed her in a rib-crushing hug.

Marcie offered her hand to Ken, which he glared at. A Canadian would have shaken it with a thin pretense of good will—and stayed sober long enough to have played decently.

"You cheat!" Ken accused.

"How?"

"An American would have just taken high ball. I sank that blue."

"I checked with the official. Table was open. By the rules."

"You two really do belong together." Ken wagged his finger back and forth between her and Emilio. "You're both a couple of crooks. If I woulda been sober, I woulda kicked your ass." Ken poked his finger at Marcie's chest.

"I didn't force a drop down your throat."

The cops walked in. Marcie's legs turned to jelly. Her upper body went stiff.

"What?" Emilio noticed her sudden rigor mortis.

He hadn't seen the cops? But they simply sat down and stared up at a TV; they weren't here to arrest her and Emilio for passing counterfeit money or waving a gun around in St. Petersburg. The waitress brought the cops coffees. Marcie relaxed.

As soon as they left, Chrissy pounced. "You stole my money. Ken owed me that from what he lost at poker."

"Don't let her bully you into giving her a cent of it," Emilio warned.

"You stay out of this. Thieves of a feather," she practically spat and stormed off.

"Let's go." Emilio pulled Marcie outside to where his three girls were sitting alone in the car. Emilio opened the driver's door. "This is Cindy, Sabrina, and Samantha. This here's Marcie, a neighbour of Uncle Abe and Uncle Jim. Daddy's going to give her a ride home."

So his marriage wasn't the sham he'd tried passing it off as, or he wouldn't be lying about who she was to his kids.

"Marcie's new here, from Canada. Do you know where that is?"

The silence probably meant no.

"Since she doesn't know anyone here, hardly, Daddy thought he'd bring her along to Uncle Ed's for Halloween."

Marcie looked at him with raised eyebrows.

"What are you going as?" the youngest asked.

"I haven't thought about it," Marcie answered.

"You haven't?"

Inconceivable, that someone hadn't yet planned her Halloween costume by the end of September. They all started telling her about theirs, and that, "Mom and Dad are going as Caesar and Cleopatra."

"That'll be very interesting," Marcie commented. Not the costumes, but Emilio bringing his wife and his mistress to the same party.

When they got to Palm Grove, Emilio let her out at the gate, only this time with no kissing goodbye. If she had a phone, she could call him and ask what the hell? Instead, she'd have to wait until the next time he turned up.

Too late to paint, instead of going home, where she'd be plagued by nightmares and cockroaches, Marcie cut across the pool to Joe's and turned the thermostat up to the legal eighty, hoping for a more peaceful night.

Marcie woke up refreshed. No work-mares, bug-mares, or bugs. On the way home, still wearing her new, even dirtier by now, white dress, she stopped by the office to mention her cockroaches and was told she'd be contacted once a date had been set with the exterminator.

After breakfast, a shower, and a change of clothes, she started a painting of Emilio, using the pictures she'd taken of him at the restaurant as references. Over the next couple of days, she finished Abe in the lamplight. Then, around noon, she went out for some sun by the pool—and saw Tim! Sitting at an umbrella table, reading a newspaper, and eating his lunch.

"What are you doing home in the middle of the day during the week?" Marcie happily plunked down in a chair beside him.

"Sometimes I gotta get away from the garage for a bit." He gulped down some milk. "I hear you're quite the pool shark. Chrissy's madder 'n all hell. At least second place ought to shut Ken up for a while. Losin' to a girl."

Tim grinned. "Though now we'll have to listen to him makin' excuses for himself."

"He blames me 'cause he was drunk."

"Sounds like him." Tim shoved in the last bite of his sandwich. "So you and Emilio are an item now, huh?"

Marcie closed her eyes. Of course, Tim had found out. "Only because I can't be with you."

"Couldn't you have picked a better second choice?" Tim joked. "And I can't change my mind now. Shitty as it is, I value my life."

Another person who feared getting shot. "We could move someplace else. You and me. If you're ever serious about changing your mind."

"I promised my boss I'd stay and work off all my fuck-ups he had to cover from before. When I was drinkin'. And anybody I worked for before him, I fucked over so bad, there's no way in hell any a them would give me a decent reference. So I'm stuck here."

"You're talented. You could prove yourself."

"With my history of being unstable? Not showin' up for work? Messin' up engines? Havin' to redo 'em on my better days 'steada takin' on new jobs, costing the shop money? Employers don't want that. I need to establish a good record here first and I owe him."

"You could start your own business."

"With what? You need capital, and there's no way in hell I qualify for a loan. And you'd be no help. No offence, but a non-working, non-American?"

Not the time to remind him that if he married her, she could work, because what job could she do that showed enough income on paper to help him get a loan? Tips didn't count at the bank. In despair, she stared at the strong lines of Tim's profile, wisps of blond hair hanging over his forehead. "Can I take a picture of you to paint?"

"What, *Stick Man Eatin' by Pool*?" Tim grinned.

"I like your body. Everything about you." Marcie took out her camera.

"I know you do. And you shouldn't. For one more reason now."

And she couldn't with any confidence say Emilio wouldn't find out. Especially since he was approaching the pool.

"Well, isn't this cozy." Emilio strolled on scene.

"Hey, man." Tim leapt up. "I ain't stealin' your girlfriend." Tim picked up his dishes and bolted for the pool gate, leaving his newspaper behind.

"A brave man," Emilio ridiculed. "Is there anything goin' on between you two I should know about?"

"No, but so what if there was? You're married. And the way you introduced me to the girls, it doesn't sound like an on-paper-only thing."

"That's part of keeping up the appearance. What do you want me to say? *This is my girlfriend?* They don't know Penny and I aren't having sex. We sleep in the same bed. That's all they have to know."

"I'm not sleeping with Tim."

"Only 'cause he's on too many drugs to get it up and he knows it. Otherwise . . ."

"What kind of 'appearance' is bringing me and your wife to the same *family* Halloween party?"

"My family knows my situation and won't say anything to the girls. Besides, she's working."

"Your kids don't seem to think so."

"That's what we go as every year. And she hasn't told 'em yet."

Marcie shrugged. "You know what you're doing. You picking Abe up for work?"

"Yeah."

"Okay, well . . ." *Have a good day. Don't shoot anyone. Or get shot. Or arrested.* Things which would make a gangster's day good.

"I'll call you la— You don't have a phone yet, do you?" he remembered.

"No."

"Go get one." He peeled a hundred off his roll and slapped it down on the table, and it stayed. Not a breeze blew. He wrote his number on the top of Tim's paper, then hugged and kissed her goodbye.

Marcie examined the bill. Not that she knew what a US hundred was supposed to look or feel like. Likely something like this, or his scam wouldn't be working. If busted for passing a fake, she could always feign ignorance. How would a Canadian be able to spot phony American money?

Marcie opened and flipped through Tim's abandoned paper. Mostly palaver about the upcoming election. A page about another bridge construction disaster in Tampa, different from the one Stan showed her in Clearwater. This one involved sinking pilings erected for an overpass which now couldn't be built, at a price tag of sixty-four million, for which nobody took responsibility. The engineers blamed the architectural firm, which in turn pointed fingers at building codes; city hall accused inspectors of closing their eyes for graft; and inspectors pilloried the unions for lacking control over labor—spelled with no *u*. Though, how, a union spokesman countered, could the union have any influence over non-union migrant workers, which contractors hired to lower costs, so the bosses could pocket the extra? The foreign scabs defended themselves by testifying that site managers made them rush work and cheaped out on materials so they, trained professionals in their own countries, couldn't adequately do the jobs they were hired for. The foremen passed the buck to the sub-contractors, under pressure to look profitable so they'd be able to competitively bid on future jobs.

All one big mess. Marcie shook her head and turned more pages. Another article about embezzlement in city hall, a big accident on the interstate, two shootings, but, most importantly, no gas station robberies, nothing involving flimflamming or counterfeit money, and no reported gun waving incidents in St. Petersburg.

Relieved, Marcie closed the paper, ripped off Emilio's phone number, and noted with incredulity that the forecast was calling for thundershowers. Today? She looked up at the blue sky with not a cloud in it.

After some painting and a nap, Marcie, seeing a huge purple bird flying toward the duck pond, wandered over to photograph the bird.

It had to have stood four feet tall, and would be way more interesting to draw for a children's book than a cat. Its mate approached from the sky, wings spread like some evil pterodactyl, as it glided down and flapped to a stop. As the bird waded knee-deep into the water, an idea for a children's book came to her: *Conrad the Crane.* Writing *and* illustrating, she'd make over twice the money she made just illustrating. She wouldn't be stealing an idea from Dennis. The birds would be all hers. The publisher was already familiar with her work, and Dennis didn't have a monopoly on the writing of children's books.

Using a page from her purse-sized sketch pad, she scribbled, Conrad Crane caroused . . . No. Not for kids. Conrad Crane caught some . . . fish? But fish didn't start with the letter *c*. Crabs. The double entendre might entertain the adults reading the story to their kids. Crustaceans? Too hard for kids. Cockroaches! Repulsive and authentic enough, which could drive the cranes to leave their country. So, Conrad Crane caught some cockroaches for lunch. No, breakfast, because that had a *c* sound in the middle. Then what? A synonym for "stood around doing nothing" because that's what these birds seemed to do. Contemplated! He contemplated his existence. No, his condition. This was fun. He'd have to come to the conclusion he couldn't take it anymore, maybe because of the hurricanes—that had a *c* in it. That could launch the action—the journey that kids' book characters always embarked on, like Dodger the Dog running away. Also, Conrad could come to the conclusion that the food sucked. He'd need to find some place too cold for cockroaches and hurricanes, like *Canada*. Obviously. He'd need a travelling companion. Cathy Cormorant! The couple could connive a plan to commence a new colony in the cooler climate. Too corpulent to fly, because, sick of cockroaches, they constantly consumed copious quantities of cookies and cupcakes, they would catch a ride on a coach—one of those fancy highway buses that their drivers didn't like calling "buses" because then they'd be bus drivers and that sounded low, like *waitresses,* so they preferred being "coach operators," which carried more dignity, like *servers*—until someone asked what a coach was, and then made the translation: "Oh. You're a bus driver." Just like *server* always got converted back into *waitress.*

So, the cranes would ride until they shed a few kilograms. They'd keep their heads low to clear overpasses. In Kansas, they could go on a crash diet of corn. In Calgary, they'd camp out on the college campus and cry into handkerchiefs, because of the fucking—no, not for kids—cursed cold. Then, at the end, they'd creep into the cafeteria and call their friends in Clearwater and proclaim they were coming home before they became a couple of cadavers.

"Trying to hide?" Ken approached the pond.

"Just writing down some ideas for a children's book."

Ken snooped over her shoulder. "I thought you were the illustrator."

"No law says I can't be an author, too, just because I mostly paint."

"No law that says you can't enter a pool tournament, either."

"I didn't think Americans had a problem with some good, old-fashioned, healthy, red-blooded competition. Isn't that what you guys are all about? Or only if you win?"

Ken glared.

"Hey. Nobody told me about any minimum blood alcohol content requirement."

"Very funny. I'm sober now. So, you think you can play? Let's go. Thousand bucks."

"What if I win again? How are you going to pay? You already owe Chrissy."

"That's my problem, okay?"

"What are you guys arguing about?" Jim emerged through the reeds.

"This ain't over," Ken promised. "We'll talk more later. Thanks to you, I have to go to work."

"Most of us who aren't gigolos do," Jim called after him. "And I'm on my way to freeze my ass at the airport. Just heard you guys out here and thought I'd come by and say hi."

"And by the way." Ken turned around and pointed at the purple birds. "Those are herons."

"Are they?" She looked at Jim.

"There are cranes in Florida"—he shrugged—"but those ain't them. Hey, Abe wants to know when he can have his painting."

"It's done."

"Come by later, after Emilio drops him off, before he has a chance to spend all his pay."

At least Jim didn't say *fake money.*

After showering, Marcie set off for the electronics place down the highway. Upon entering the store, she saw the phones right away, on display right at the front. She selected the cheapest, then got the salesman to explain the basics of using it before heading for the cashier to pay. Without blinking, the girl took Emilio's hundred and handed Marcie the change. No problem. Guessing Emilio would probably ask for it, she kept it separate from her own cash and headed outside, excited to play around with her first cell phone.

In case she had problems, Marcie stayed close to the store, so she could run in for help if she needed it. To sit, she perched on a power pole, likely downed in the last hurricane, and turned her back to the sun, so her body's shadow covered the phone's screen, enabling her to see what was on it. To try out text messaging, she punched in Emilio's number, then hit the 4 four times for an *I*, the 0 twice for a space, the 4 again three times for an *H*, the 2 only twice for an *A*, and so on until she spelled out, I HAVE A CELL PHONE, then hit the green bracket to send. A little tedious, but kind of fun. Now Emilio would have her number and she didn't have to worry about interrupting him in the middle of something, like a possible robbery, as she could have by calling at the wrong moment. This way, he could read the message when he was able.

Then, she dialled Dennis! Finally. After a month. He'd be freaking.

Four-thirty, Marcie checked her watch. In Calgary— Mountain Daylight Time—he'd be finishing dinner.

She listened to the ring tone in her ear. Kind of trippy, using a phone from outside. Though how long had she been here? Because she noticed it had suddenly become very dark. Odd, because, though dusk was falling earlier, it stayed light until at least six. Unless her watch had stopped. But it had been light a minute ago. She looked up at the sky, which had turned an angry grey. Thunder rumbled. A drop of hot rain fell on her face before the sky opened. A terrible racket ensued, as sheets of water cascaded onto the store's metal awning. Cackling at being suddenly soaked with hot water, she dropped the phone in her purse for its protection and stood in the deluge, never having experienced rain warmer than freezing cold. In Calgary, the thermometer dropped to about three degrees above zero Celsius whenever it rained. Here, it remained ninety-five Fahrenheit, causing steam to billow up from the asphalt, creating one very large shower, the spray resembling rice more than rain.

Then it was over. In less than five minutes, the blue sky returned. In moments, the sun evaporated all traces of the tropical cloudburst, as if the squall had never happened.

As she walked home, her purse erupted in song and flashing lights. Her phone! She reached for it and poked at the green symbol to answer. "Hello?"

"About damn time I heard from you!"

"Dennis!"

"And what the hell was all that noise?"

"A thunderstorm. It was really weird. It came out of nowhere and the temperature stayed ninety-five!"

"Yeah, well, lucky you. It's minus fifteen here with the windchill."

Marcie shuddered. "Sorry I haven't called sooner. I've been busy and I just got a phone. I got email too, so I can send you what I've come up with for *Tom*."

"Tim," Dennis corrected. "But I haven't sent you the storyline."

"They're just some drawings of a cat. My neighbour Tim has one. I thought maybe we could set the story down here."

"No. It's set at the Stampede. Okay. Well, I wish I could talk, but I gotta run and take the kids to piano."

"Okay. Later then." Marcie hit the key with the red symbol to end the call.

After dinner, she delivered Abe's painting to Abe and collected three hundred real or fake dollars. The rest of the evening she painted the real Tim, not Dennis's cat, reading the paper by the pool, sunglasses on his head, wispy blond hair blowing in the breeze, and hung the finished canvas in her walk-in closet, so Emilio wouldn't be likely to see it. A tear fell. Why did one person always feel something so powerfully and the other, often nothing at all? Or wouldn't allow themselves to act on their feelings for logical-only-to-them reasons? Because Tim did feel something.

Too tired to care about cockroaches, Marcie shuffled to her mattress and quickly fell asleep, fantasizing about Tim. And didn't dream about restaurants. Hopefully, another pattern broken.

4. October

Emilio banged on her door in the morning. "Where were you last night?"

"Here."

"You didn't answer the phone when I called."

"I must have slept through it."

"Why weren't you at Joe's?" he demanded.

"I fell asleep painting."

"Me?"

"I haven't started yours yet. Oh. Here." She gave him the change from her phone purchase. He then invited her to the aquarium later.

"I promised the girls I'd take 'em after school."

"Sure." She might get some interesting pictures for the *Tim/Tom* book. Cats liked fish. And if Dennis persisted in wanting his set at the Stampede, who said she couldn't do a cat book on her own?

Which reminded her. "Is there an internet café around here?"

"The copy place sells computer time by the hour. If you can be ready by the time Abe is, I'll drop you off."

Marcie hurried to change and put on makeup.

When she logged into her email account after Emilio dropped her off at the copy place, she found a message from Stan. "Hope you got home okay. I'll call you next time I'm in your vicinity."

She sent Dennis an email then wrote back to Stan. Or, at least, opened an e-letter and stared at the blank electronic page. How to tell him she'd love to see him, but not in Tampa. Emilio could kill them. She should just tell Stan she was seeing someone. He was married and lived far away, so he'd understand the need for secrecy and couldn't expect her not to be seeing anyone. How delighted would he be if she showed up in California, where he lived? Maybe she could suggest they meet in a city close by. Like . . . she'd have to look at a map. Somewhere other than Clearwater or St. Petersburg—places Emilio went.

An electronic blip indicated an incoming email. From Dennis. With the *Tim* storyline, set in Calgary, a place she'd had enough of and didn't look forward to illustrating. "What about having Tom's family drive to Florida on spring break?" she counter-suggested. Something very Canadian. "Let me put together some sketches."

She logged off the computer and, on the way home, stopped at a bank, where she was told she couldn't open an account without a social security number, a work visa, or a green card. She almost pulled out one of the bills Abe had given her to ask if it was real. But what if it wasn't? Could the police come to arrest her right there in the bank? Also, she'd lose several hundred dollars. She was better off not knowing, so she could try to pawn them off on somebody else.

To hold the money—real or illegal—that she was earning from her art, she bought a strong box at an office supply store.

Once back home, she stopped in at the rental office and left her new phone number, so she could be more conveniently notified when the exterminator would be coming around.

She then made mid-afternoon lunch, ate on her lanai, showered, brushed her teeth, and dressed for an evening at the aquarium. Until Emilio came by, she sketched her ideas for *Tom* and worked on *Conrad*. She added little maple leaf ear-muffs where the cranes' ears would be, then surrounded them with a flock of Canada geese, even though most of those flew south for the winter. Some stayed and lived off handouts from people, despite posted mandates not to feed wildlife.

When she heard Emilio's car, Marcie grabbed a copy of *Dodger the Dog* and ran out to meet him.

"Marcie painted the pictures," Emilio explained to them. "See her name on the cover, where it says, *Illustrated by*?"

"Are you famous?" one of his girls asked.

"She is." Emilio answered before Marcie could. "So y'all have to be on your best behaviour. Or she'll write a book about three naughty girls."

Marcie sat silent. Emilio didn't start a conversation, either, but at least the trip wasn't quiet because the girls were all reading *Dodger the Dog* to each other and laughing.

Emilio paid their way in with a hundred.

"Check this out." Emilio pointed at a six-foot-long grouper fish. "Tell me that ain't the ugliest mother."

Marcie photographed it. A fish the same size as a human would scare the shit out of a cat. Her other favourite: a self-propelling seahorse that looked like a plant with eyes, which she snapped a picture of also, along with baby gators and crocs, and the petting tank filled with sea anemones and starfish.

After Emilio dropped her off at home, she started cat sketches for Dennis, then spent the night at Joe's in case

Emilio called her there to check up on her, even though she had her own phone.

But Emilio didn't call. In the morning, she made Joe's bed and went home for breakfast, after which, for exercise, she walked through neighbourhoods decorated for Halloween and photographed witches tacked onto palm trees and jack-o-lanterns leering from tropical gardens. The owners of one house had placed the severed head of a doll and its decapitated body on either side of a parked car's tire, with a gruesomely realistic effect. Sheet ghosts made by humans dangled alongside nature's gauze specters high up in Spanish moss trees, adding an extra haunting effect. The still-boarded-up windows from the recent hurricane season were the crowning, disturbing touch.

Almost as surreal, a bicycle shop appeared in this sinister tropical paradise. A bike would be great for exercise and getting around faster. Marcie noted the address and came back the next day with cash. She chose a good used twenty-one speed with a basket and hoped the guy didn't look too close at the currency.

In her aimless cycling around on a very circuitous way home, Marcie came upon Tampa Bay, fronted by wide, empty sidewalks no one cycled, skateboarded, or walked along. The deserted sight gave her the impression of having survived one of those neutron bombs she'd feared as a kid, the ones rumoured to kill all the people and leave the buildings standing. In Calgary, any bike path along water drew a congestion of fitness freaks, even on crappy days. The only people riding bikes here were derelicts—men who'd lost their driver's licences too many times. People with whom she'd be lumped.

She gaped at and photographed the mansions across the wide road, then turned onto some side streets with even larger and more opulent homes. One even took up a whole square city block.

Her route led her farther south toward the airbase—into a shocking display of Third World poverty! Clotheslines weighted with laundry sagged between shacks. Cliché car wrecks balanced on cement blocks sat surrounded by tall grass. Quonset huts, which she knew only from movies, completed a picture of what she would have expected to find somewhere in Africa, but was staring right back at her, here, in the U.S. of A.—the land of the gun-toting free, and home of the capitalist brave. But at least these poor people had places to live, unlike the homeless who slept on the streets of downtown Canadian cities. Or maybe the impoverished did that here too; she hadn't yet toured Tampa's downtown.

Thirsty, she stopped in a convenience store and bought a water. She then headed north and came across the mall near her place, where she'd driven Emilio's car so she could buy brunch clothes. With the afternoon to kill, she locked her bike to a tree—not that anyone who shopped here would steal anything self-propelled—and climbed the steps to explore the cobble-stoned upper terrace. It was like entering a whole other world. Waiflike fashion models swarmed around fountains and bobbed in and out of fine restaurants, their tiny hands weighted by diamond rings and fake nails, clutching both drinks and cell phones—the Tampa equivalent of ladies who lunched, only these were all young. Other molls? Emilio was hardly keeping her in that style, but still, she felt rich, sweating in shorts in October and not working. And to be sitting among so much opulence! To attain it herself, she'd have to sell a hell of a lot of paintings and copies of *Dodger the Dog*. Or maybe Joe would deck her out like that. Really, what was the danger of marrying someone who'd done time in jail? In the movies, the wives and girlfriends of mobsters didn't get hauled off with their husbands and boyfriends. Marcie perched on the edge of an elaborate rock fountain surrounded by palm trees and banana leaves, and continued to soak in the scene outside. Why freeze in the air conditioning?

The ring tone of her phone startled her out of her reverie. *Emilio*, she read the screen's call display.

"Where are you?" his voice boomed in her ear when she answered.

"At the mall."

"I got a couple hours this evening. The girls have gymnastics. Meet me at Joe's around seven." He hung up before she could answer. Maybe the women around here were taking the same sorts of calls on their phones. Call girls. Straddling the fine line between professional sex workers and girlfriends getting gifts.

At five to seven, freshly showered and changed, she cut through the pool over to Joe's, where she stayed after Emilio left, and slept very well, either because of the sex or the exercise on the bicycle.

In the morning, she noticed a ghetto blaster—battery operated. Why hadn't she seen it before? Music to paint by! They—Emilio and Joe—shouldn't mind if she borrowed it. She grabbed a random handful of CDs and brought them and the stereo out to the pool and left them while she ran into her place to grab her sketchbook. When she returned, she opened to a fresh page, popped in a CD, and pressed Play. Nothing happened. Dead batteries, probably. She opened the hatch to see what kind it needed, but instead of batteries, bags of white powder popped out. *Aw, shit.*

And more shit. Ken approached. Under pressure, she'd never get the bags back in the compartment without puncturing at least one. So, instead, she gently set the portable stereo overtop of the bags, hoping its weight wouldn't break them all open and that Ken wouldn't touch it.

"Next Friday," he snarled.

"What?"

"Don't play dumb. You know what."

"I never agreed to a rematch."

"Then you're a thief, just like your boyfriend."

"Winning a tournament isn't theft, but, okay, fine. I could use another thousand dollars," Marcie bluffed, hoping to scare him off with bravado. "Where and what time?"

Instead of declining, he stated, "Six o'clock." And gave her the address of a pool hall. "And, you can let your boyfriend know that if he hits my store with one of his phony hundreds, he's a dead man."

"I'll pass that on. Which store's that?"

"He'll see me. And when he does, if he doesn't turn around and hightail it, I'm calling the cops. And you can tell him that, too."

When Ken left, she lifted the radio and breathed a sigh of relief at the sight of the still-intact bags. Preferring not to try stuffing the baggies back in when any of the surrounding neighbours could be watching from their windows, she slipped the drugs into her purse, casually picked up the radio, and walked back to Joe's. She couldn't keep sitting by the pool, not listening to music while having a radio in front of her. Someone would come along and ask questions. Or try turning it on.

Whose coke was it? Whose radio? Did Emilio hide his coke in Joe's radio or had Emilio brought his own radio over to Joe's to keep his wife and kids from finding it? Or, was Joe holding out on Emilio, having hidden his own stash of coke in his own radio before being dragged off to jail? Or, were the two of them, in conjunction, stuffing coke in the lingerie, instead of the underwear already being narc'd up in Puerto Rico? Did it matter? Yes. Because to whom should she confess her honest mistake without risking ratting out one man to the other, should one of them realize his radio had been monkeyed with? Only the owner of it would notice any disturbance if she couldn't get the bags in exactly the way they had been, so she'd admit responsibility only to whichever man spoke to her about it. But then, Emilio would wonder why she hadn't said something to him first, causing him to question her loyalty, and she didn't want a man carrying a gun suspecting her of some kind of treason. *I didn't think it'd be a big deal,* she could honestly say, because if she could restore the bags without damage, not one gram would be missing.

Marcie sat down on the couch with the coke, the bags, and the ghetto blaster. Fifteen minutes later, she had all the bags back inside. Sweating, she replaced the radio and dusted the whole apartment, then collected her art supplies on her way home, because for the rest of the day, her time would be better spent practicing pool than painting.

She looked up the address Ken had given her on her map and cycled there. The ride helped dissipate some of her stress over the coke bags, though practicing while still agitated would be great preparation for the real match with Ken, because she'd be plenty stressed over the possibility of losing one month in Florida.

She locked up her bike—because the people here, unlike at the mall, really might steal her wheels—and paid for table time with one of Emilio's hundreds he'd given her in payment for the painting of him. A good test of the bill's authenticity, because pool hall attendants would be more likely to be on the lookout for counterfeit money. This guy seemed to notice nothing amiss and gave her change and some balls.

"Also," Marcie asked, "do you sell used cues?" Because what if Ken knew people here and paid them to hide all the choice nineteens on match day?

The man showed her a wide selection; Marcie selected her favourite, which he said she could try first.

While she was practicing, her phone rang. *Emilio.* Lovely. He'd hear the background noise of clicking pool balls and know where she was, then yell at her for agreeing to a rematch with Ken, because why else would she be at a pool hall? So, she ignored the ringing, which further toughened her nerves against distractions, and called Emilio back when she was done.

"Hi. Sorry, I didn't hear the phone when you called."

"Where were you?"

"Out on my bike."

"When'd you get a bike?"

"Yesterday."

"You never told me."

"I figured you'd see it eventually."

"Anyway, I thought I'd come by for a bit, once the girls fell asleep."

"Sure. I'm just on my way home."

She arrived as Emilio drove through the gate. "Perfect timing." He grinned and parked the car.

But it wasn't. Aside from reeking of cigarette smoke, she carried a pool cue. Which he noticed.

"That motherfucker bullied you into a rematch, didn't he? I knew he would! That's why you didn't answer your phone. Fine. You want to play him, that's your business. Just make damn sure he puts the money up front, or you don't play."

Marcie nodded.

"When is this rematch?"

"Next Friday at six."

"And make sure there's a referee."

Probably good advice. Marcie wheeled the bike into her suite. "My place or Joe's?"

"Here's good. But take a shower first."

***

In the morning, the office called to say the fumigators would be by around noon and advised her she should make plans to be out for about six hours. She painted Halloween houses by the pool and used Joe's bathroom when she needed to go.

Seven hours later, she brought the canvases into her own place, grabbed some cash, and pedalled off to the pool hall again. None of the men there offered her any free lessons. Either, at thirty, she'd become less appealing, or they thought they had nothing to teach her. Yet still she watched them play, hoping whatever skills they possessed and she didn't would pour in by osmosis.

Each evening, she bought time on a different table so she'd know each one's speed and surface, so none would be unfamiliar no matter which one Ken picked or was available on rematch night. She read magazine articles on setting up shots and practiced bottom spins to bring the cue ball back to where she wanted it. She systematically put various degrees of strength into her shots and observed the results. One day, she shot at only the eight to make sure she wouldn't choke on it, placing it both with other balls and by itself.

Afternoons, she still painted, finishing three Halloween houses.

Thursday, Ken came by to remind her of their rematch. Marcie didn't remind Emilio of it, but Friday night, dressed in his pink suit, he showed up in plenty of time to drive her to the pool hall. Marcie wore jeans instead of shorts; the evenings were getting cooler.

The pool hall was packed, but not many people were playing. Could they all have come watch her and Ken's grudge match? Ken must be well known here, or she, by winning the bar tournament, had become famous. She requested a referee for the game. The table was already set up. Marcie assembled and chalked her cue. And waited. Ten minutes to the hour and Ken hadn't showed.

At two minutes to six, Ken—still wearing his company shirt—and his entourage blew in. He looked rattled from being rushed or from drinking too much coffee on his shift, putting him at the opposite end of the nervous spectrum from when he'd played her before. Better yet, for her, he ordered a cola! Such an elevated heart rate would throw off his game, especially since he usually played half-inebriated. Was he stupid?

Marcie counted out a thousand dollars in twenties in front of the proprietor—she'd gone to the bank and made a cash withdrawal from her account still in Canada—and waited for Ken to do likewise, then they made their way to the table. The ref tossed the coin. As it came down, Ken asked, "Who the hell's this?"

"The ref," Marcie stated. "And I'm guessing most audience here know the rules. So . . ." *Don't even try cheating or accusing me of it.* The unspoken message seemed to be received loud and clear.

The ref re-tossed the coin. "Tails," she called first. "If you have no objection, since I'm your invited guest."

"Since it's heads—" Ken peeked—"no."

Marcie turned over the quarter to make sure it had two different sides.

Ken screwed together his cue, then noticed hers. "You've been practicing!" Ken concluded.

"Is there a rule against that?" Marcie challenged.

Ken fumed. "I've been working. You have nothing else to do all day."

"You knew that before challenging me to the rematch. What'd you think I'd do? But, at least you won break, since you think you're so handicapped. So you can run the table and beat me, because," she reminded him, "you're sober now. And, just so you don't forget, we're only playing one game. So make it count."

Ken lit a cigarette, as if his heart wouldn't be racing fast enough already. All the bicycling had brought Marcie's heart rate down. Better for keeping her hands steady. Ken bent over and lined up his shot—without chalking! Marcie held her breath, hoping he wouldn't remember at the last minute. He didn't, and slammed the shiny metal cue tip into the cue ball. And scratched.

Marcie smirked. "By some rules, that could have been game right now." But instead of claiming a win, she graciously offered him chalk.

Ken grabbed it and rammed the cube of blue powder onto his cue tip, twisting it aggressively before once again lining up for his break, which shattered the triangle of balls. A low ball dribbled in. He missed his next shot. "Just to clarify," Marcie checked with the official, "table's still open?"

"Yeah." He shrugged, like any idiot would know that.

Marcie looked at Ken then ran the table, but missed on the eight ball. A potentially fatal mistake, if Ken was on his game, but that didn't seem likely. He put down two high balls, but used too much power on his third, causing a ricochet. "Fuck!" he quietly snarled, slamming the rubber end of his cue into the floor.

Marcie lined up the eight, like she'd been doing all week. Kept her hand steady, and gently shot. It seemed to pause on the lip of the pocket, then dropped.

Ken swore profusely. Most of the pool hall cheered.

"That's my girl!" Emilio scooped her up in a rib-crushing hug. Then collected a lot of money. "You just made me a rich man." He slipped her a few hundred before escorting her over to collect Ken's thousand, and hers. Two more months in Florida!

Some large men who worked at the pool hall kept an eye on Ken to make sure he left without kicking anything.

In the morning, someone knocked on her door. Assuming it'd be Emilio, she answered without bothering to dress. Instead of a five-foot-seven Hispanic dude, a seven-foot monster with lighted-up yellow eyes stood in the doorway. Ken jumped out from behind his costume. Marcie slammed the door.

"I need a favour," Ken called.

Like that would make her open the door, though, she supposed he wouldn't go away until she did. And she was curious about what this favour could be. "Just let me dress." She tied on her robe and opened the door.

"Chrissy threw me out, thanks to you, so I need a place to stay."

"And you think I'll let you stay here?"

"You owe me!"

"Like hell!"

"Come on. You spend half your nights at Joe's anyways. Just till I find a place."

"Like you'd look. Or could afford one if you can't pay half for the one you already have. Had," Marcie corrected.

"Come on," Ken implored. "Friends help friends."

Friends? Marcie's mouth dropped.

"At least let me leave my costume here. It's my only chance o' payin' Chrissy back."

"How? Someone's going to give you two thousand dollars for that?" Marcie questioned.

"If I win first place, yeah."

"Where?"

"Like I'd tell you."

"Don't worry. I'm not going to build a costume," Marcie assured him. "And I already have plans for Halloween. I was just curious."

"So?"

"All right. Leave him." Marcie pointed to an empty corner, where the gleaming yellow eyes couldn't be seen if she had to get up in the middle of the night to use the bathroom.

"Thanks." Ken propped his prize up against the wall, where it slumped like a giant puppet.

Americans sure got into Halloween. In Calgary, nobody made a big deal of it. A few of the bars threw costume parties, the kids trick-or-treated, and that was about it. No one went to a lot of trouble, and if a anyone offered a prize for a costume, it wouldn't have been anything significant. Maybe a few free passes to something or free booze or food.

Which gave her an idea. If Americans so valued Halloween, those homes she painted might be worth something to the home owners.

When Ken left, she rifled through her photographs to see if she picked up the street sign in the background. Yes! She cycled to the copy store and typed up a letter.

Hi. Enclosed is a picture of a painting I did of your house decorated for Halloween. I was wondering if you'd like to purchase the original canvas for three hundred dollars. The price Jim, Abe, and Emilio had paid for theirs. Or, should she charge less? Maybe two hundred. Better to go low and feel out the market. *"This isn't extortion or anything. I'm just an artist, hoping to sell some of my work. If you don't want to buy, that's fine. I'm not going to do anything, like wreck your house. Call me, and we can arrange a time and place to meet."*

She typed in her phone number, signed her name, and printed three copies, one for the owner of each house from which each completed painting had come. She printed off a photograph of each one of the paintings, bought three stamps and three envelopes, and addressed them. "Do you have a book of zip codes?" she asked the clerk, because in Canada, there was a book of postal codes.

She put the letters together with the photographs, and dropped them in the mail. Hopefully, they'd arrive before Halloween. If this worked, she could do the same thing at Christmas and when she saw For Sale signs in yards. If people were moving, they might like a memento of their former home. Or, the Realtor might like to give a gift to the purchaser. One house, two potential buyers.

While in the copy shop, she read an email from Dennis, kiboshing her spring break idea for his book. Fine, she'd do her own book. She promised him she'd get on the Stampede sketches.

The rest of the day, she cycled around, photographing houses for sale, and bought some more canvases.

That night, just after she'd fallen asleep, a knock on her door woke her. Ken couldn't be wanting his costume already. Emilio again? She grabbed a robe. "Who is it?"

"Pat."

Pat? She opened the door. Pat stood holding a pillow and blankets. "I can't sleep with his snoring."

"Whose?"

"Ken's. Thanks to you, he's moved onto my couch. Chrissy threw him out."

"So he said when he came by." Marcie pointed at Ken's costume.

"He wore that last year! He's not going to win again with the same one."

"He thinks otherwise. So if he's at your place," Marcie reasoned, "why didn't he bring it there?"

"Probably because he came here first, figuring he'd guilt you into letting him stay, and when you wouldn't, thought couch surfing would be easier empty-handed. Emilio here?" Pat looked around.

"You'd know if he was."

"Probably, yeah. So? You gonna invite me in?"

"You want to sleep on the floor?"

"I was thinking you could spend the night at Joe's and I could sleep on your air mattress. I have to work in the morning."

"Why don't you go by Tim's and borrow some of his sleeping pills?"

"I don't want to become a drug addict, too. I drink too much already."

"Tell Ken he can't stay."

"I can't turn my back on a friend."

"Well, I'm not going over to Joe's. I'm tired. So, floor or nothing."

"We could share."

"Like I'd trust you to stay on your side," she said, even though she knew he would. How did she know she wouldn't find Pat in bed with her by morning? Because he, like everyone else, didn't want to get shot, and he couldn't be sure she wouldn't mention the incident to Emilio. "Floor or nothing."

"Floor, then," Pat agreed.

Pat had gone by the time she woke up, but his blankets, neatly folded in front of Ken's costume, remained, indicating his intended return.

After breakfast, she settled on the lanai to work on her version of *Tom the Tomcat,* then after lunch, moved camp to the pool, where Emilio found her. "Got your costume yet?"

"No."

He kissed her. "Pack up. Grab your purse. I'll drop you off at the costume store." He picked up some canvases and helped her carry them inside. Then glared at the blankets. "You're letting Ken stay here?"

"Those are Pat's. He couldn't sleep with Ken's snoring. Ken's just leaving his costume here."

"That's bullshit."

"Which?"

"Both. You shouldn't let people walk over you like that. You want me to take care of this?"

"No!"

"Why don't you move into Joe's? Sell your lease to Pat."

"Like Pat could afford rent in two places, plus pay for the house that his wife's in, because Ken hasn't got money to pay Pat for rent. And what if Joe doesn't want me for a wife but is stuck with me and all my stuff in his place till I can move out?"

"He's never there anyway, and then you'd have the money to find another apartment."

"Only supposing Pat pays me, because I've paid for this place till the end of February. Besides, Joe's has no room for me to paint or for my bike, which I wouldn't want to haul up and down three flights of stairs anyway."

"What about when you're married?"

"Then we could find a two-bedroom on a ground floor, if he agrees to the idea and we get along. But I'm not moving into the home of some man I've never met when I feel more comfortable here."

"Suit yourself." Emilio shrugged.

Once inside, she expected him to take her to bed. Instead, he told her to hurry up and get ready. "My girls are in the car. Professional day at school and Penny's working."

In Canada, people flipped out if somebody left a dog in the car for five minutes, never mind kids.

Emilio let her and his kids out at the costume store entrance, giving each a kiss and one hundred dollars, but instead of parking the car and walking back to join them, he drove off the property! "Hey!" she uselessly hollered into the air. Then asked the girls, "Did your dad say how long he was going to be gone?" If she phoned to ask, he wouldn't answer, because he was driving.

They shook their heads.

At least they all had something to do. For a while. "Okay. Let's go find some costumes." As a sort of revenge, Marcie chose one that consisted of, basically, scarves.

After all four had paid separately for the costumes, receiving legal tender in change, Marcie texted, WHEN R U BNMING BACK? Then corrected BNMING to COMING, frustrated with having to hit each key so many times to get the right letter.

Emilio didn't answer. Now what? The girls chased each other around the parking lot; Marcie sat on the sidewalk in front of the store. The girls joined her when they got tired and asked, "What are we going to do now?"

"I don't know. What would you like to do?" At work, she'd detested serving kids in her section, never mind being stuck babysitting for a whole afternoon. This time, Emilio wasn't getting his change, not that there was a lot of it.

Nobody had any ideas about what to do. She could call a cab and take the girls . . . where? "Let's go for a walk," Marcie suggested, hoping they might run into something entertaining, like maybe a park or a mall or even a fast-food place.

After two blocks, the girls complained they were tired and their feet hurt. There was nowhere to sit down. This city had absolutely no benches. Because here, people didn't wander around on foot. They drove. At least there were sidewalks.

"How 'bout I give you a piggyback?" Marcie offered the smallest girl. The spectacle energized her sisters into trying to give each other piggyback rides until they tired and had to sit down at the side of the road. Eventually, Marcie sat down beside them.

Eventually, a car stopped. "Are you all okay?" the driver electronically opened the passenger window and called across the passenger seat.

"Just abandoned. Do you know if there's anywhere near here to go?" Marcie asked.

"There's sort of a beach up a ways. I can drive you if you want."

The girls were climbing in the car before Marcie could say yes or no. "You wouldn't happen to have any extra water or soda or anything, would you?"

He drove them to a store first. Marcie thanked him profusely. "We haven't had anything to drink for over an hour."

The man then dropped them off at the beach.

"Again, thank you so much."

"Glad I could help. Have fun!" He drove off, having left them on a tiny stretch of sand that looked more like a small industrial waste dump.

Green-and-brown foamy water appearing too toxic even for sharks lazily lapped against the shore. At least there were rocks to sit on and some room to run. The girls took off their shoes and ran to the water's edge, where they busied themselves building sand structures. Marcie perched on a rock and watched. Then thought to photograph the girls as reference pictures for the cat book's illustrations. She scratched her butt cheeks, then hopped up and dug at the backs of her legs because they itched. And then burned. Had she sat in something? The girls were starting to scratch their legs and butts, too. Again, she texted Emilio. HOW MUBH KONGER R U GOING 2 B?

No answer came back. He was likely too busy delivering cocaine-stuffed underwear. What if he got busted? Or disappeared for some other reason? Then she'd be phoning every hospital in the Tampa Bay area, asking for Penny . . .? Her daughters should know her last name, because, Marcie realized, she didn't even know Emilio's.

After another half hour, Marcie didn't give a rat's ass if she interrupted a robbery and called Emilio, but his phone went to voice mail. "Where the hell are you? We're tired and hungry." Marcie left a message.

A few minutes later, the girls waddled over, all needing to pee. "You can go in the water or in the trees."

After another interminably long half hour passed, Emilio finally called back. "Where the hell are you? The guy at the costume store said you left two hours ago."

"You expected us to stay there and wait? We're at the beach."

"What beach? There is no beach in Tampa."

"I don't know. There's sand. And a big hydro tower."

"There?" Emilio swore and hung up.

"Daddy's coming," Marcie assured the crying girls. "We'll climb up to the side of the road and wait for him."

Finally, she heard Emilio's car. When he pulled over, everybody piled in. Silent anger hung thick in the car until Emilio couldn't help noticing all of them squirming and itching. "We must have sat in something." Marcie leaned to one side and showed him the underside of one leg.

"Sand ants. You let them sit in sand ants?" Emilio exploded.

Let them? "Like I'd know about sand ants."

"If you would have stayed in the store . . ."

"If you wouldn't have taken off . . ."

"Now there'll be blood on the upholstery."

She resisted pointing out his interior was already shit. Nobody said anything for the rest of the trip, including when she exited the car outside her gate.

Pat was waiting outside her door—with a suitcase.

"It's not bedtime," she pointed out.

"I know. Ken's on nights. So he didn't want me banging around when he was tryin' to sleep."

"How long have you been standing here?"

"Not long. I was out by the pool till I saw you get home."

Marcie unlocked her door.

"What happened to your legs?"

"Apparently I sat in some sand ants."

"Those are nasty." Pat shook his head.

"What time does Ken leave for work?"

"Around eleven, I guess. Why?"

"After he leaves, go home, call a locksmith, and have the lock changed before he gets off shift in the morning."

"I couldn't do that. Where would he go?"

"That's not your problem. Or borrow a chaise from the pool and sleep on your lanai if his snoring bothers you. Or make Ken sleep outside. And tell him too fucking bad if your banging around keeps him up. It's your place."

"I'll find someplace else to stay, if you want."

"Sorry, I'm just not used to roommates, or kids, and this rash is driving me nuts."

"There's lotion. Come on. I'll walk over to the store with you."

On their way out of the breezeway, they passed Tim coming home. Now he'd think she was sleeping with Pat. He and Tim exchanged pleasant greetings while Marcie stared off at the horizon.

Emilio phoned as they entered the store. She let it go to voicemail. Normally, men left if something went wrong—and even if it didn't. Why couldn't Emilio follow the pattern? He called back practically as soon as the phone stopped ringing the first time. On the third sequence of rings, she gave up and answered.

"Hey. I'm sorry. Penny had to work. So did I, and I didn't know what to do."

"What would you have done without me? This couldn't be the first time that's happened."

"I've done you a few favours, you know."

"I know. And I appreciate them. But I told you, I don't do kids. I don't want you thinking you can just leave me to babysit whenever . . ."

"You know why Ken was almost late for that rematch and came in lookin' all frazzled?"

Emilio was going to tell her.

"I had some guys go inta his store and buy a bunch of stuff at the last minute so he'd be held up countin' his cash before turning the till over to the next shift."

"So you didn't think I could actually beat him without help?"

"Let's say, with all the money I had riding on that game, I wanted a little extra insurance."

"Then you benefitted from me too, so who was that favour really for?"

"I gave you a share."

"I know. And thank you."

"And I bought that painting."

"Thank you for that too."

"And I'm fixing it so you can stay in the States."

"This is a very big debt I'm incurring, and I don't like owing people."

"I'm not *people*. People who are together do things for each other."

"They also should respect boundaries. I said I don't do kids, and I don't like things being held over my head."

"Got it. But, hey, the girls said they had a great time. Anyway, I just wanted to apologize."

Then he'd do the same thing again. And apologize for that too. She'd seen the pattern before. "Okay," she accepted his apology.

"See you tomorrow," he gently signed off.

At eleven, when Pat had said Ken left for work, she reminded Pat of the time, and sent him home with all his belongings. "If you don't fix this yourself, Emilio's going to. He hit the roof when he saw your blankets. Who knows what he'll do if he finds suitcases?"

"You shouldn't let that little punk control your life."

But Pat took his belongings and left.

The next morning, she opened the phone book of business listings and wrote down the names of all the children's boutiques and bookstores, along with their addresses. Then she numbered them from closest to farthest after locating them on her map. Dressed as professionally as her limited wardrobe allowed, she loaded up her bike basket with copies of *Dodger the Dog,* and set off on her bike to make inquiries.

"All our inventory has to be approved by head office," she was told at the first store.

"Do you have the head office number I could call?"

The staff person gave it to her and she called it from outside, but was told she'd have to contact the distributor. When she got that number and phoned, they said they only purchased from a select group of publishers. Marcie tried a different chain and found out it was owned by the same company and so followed the same procedure.

The manager of a large independent bookstore wasn't in. Marcie left her number.

When her phone rang on her way to the next place, it wasn't the independent store's owner, but Emilio, so she tossed the phone unanswered back in her purse, then parked in front of another independent bookseller.

"Oooooh, he's so cute!" The lady at the store fawned over *Dodger*. "We'd love to have this in our local section."

But . . .?

"We'll start with maybe half a dozen copies and I'll give you a call as they sell."

Not a rejection! Euphoric, Marcie left six copies of the book, forcing herself to calmly walk out instead of dancing.

"Have you tried the Itty-Bitty Book Worm? I bet they'd love this." The lady at the next store suggested.

"Not yet. Thank you." When she got there, Marcie mentioned, "Word on the Wall took six and Tiny Tots said I should try here."

"Aw, he's adorable. Look at the boy. This'll sell. Sure, we'll take a few. Do we order more from the publisher or go through you?"

A stellar day. She'd have to tell the publisher she was opening up the Florida market and ask if the company could distribute down here and enable her—and Dennis—to maybe get into the chains.

The owner of a run-down used bookstore in a rough neighbourhood showed less enthusiasm. "I'm not saying it's a bad book. It'd just be hard for kids around here to relate. In their world, somebody'd shoot or torture the dog, take him home and neglect him, or get him stoned. Parents 'round here would sooner buy the kid another dog if it ran away before looking all over hell and gone for the old one. More likely, they'd tell the kids they should have taken better care of it. Attachment isn't much of a concept with these people, the way everybody comes and goes, including dads and 'uncles.' Police take away family members, gangs shoot them, new partners move in. And, on top of all that, the pictures aren't of anything these kids can relate to. Big house? Snow? Hell, even an unshared backyard's a foreign concept for most of 'em."

Marcie argued, "Most TV programs show people richer than most of us could ever dream of becoming, and we watch those."

"That's different."

Though she didn't see how.

"Okay." He stared at the pictures. "It is kind of cute. I'll buy a couple copies. If they don't sell before Christmas, I could give them as gifts to my friends."

He gave her cash up front for three.

Needing to pee before heading home, she stopped at a service station to ask for the bathroom key. And saw Tim working on a car in the service bay. He worked here? Great. He was going to think she'd followed him and hate her more than he did already.

"What are you doing here?" he accused. Just as she expected, he thought she'd been stalking him.

"I was out and needed a bathroom. Sorry."

After using it, she returned the key and was about to ride off, when Tim called, "You headed home?" He emerged from behind her, minus his coveralls.

"Yeah."

"I'll ride with ya."

Marcie's heart rate almost doubled. Half euphoric, she followed Tim off the property and onto the road. At a red light, he asked, "Wanna grab something t'eat?"

What had happened? Her brain cautioned her heart against soaring too much. This wasn't really a date but a chance meeting with a neighbour, whom he had no reason to go out of his way to avoid. Maybe he felt more comfortable with her now, believing she had too many other men in her life to bother with him. Plus, he was probably hungry; she was there, so why not eat with her? Better than eating alone? That was half the reason she stayed with Emilio. Tim could be just as bored with his own company and the people at work. But, for whatever reason, he'd asked her to dinner!

"I'd love to!"

Tim led the way onto a side street, so they could ride side by side, or because that was the way to the restaurant. "See that house?" He pointed to a brick mansion with white pillars on either side of the porch and a circular driveway cutting through the immaculate expanse of green lawn.

"Yeah."

"I grew up in one of those. Up in New Jersey."

"Wow."

"My dad owned his own garage. Then started a franchise. Left it all to me when he died. I sold the business, bought the house my ex took, and pissed away the rest of the money. I didn't even travel nowhere. Hookers, drugs, booze, pickin' up tabs . . ."

Now all he had was a bike worth as much as a cheap car.

"The rest o' my family don't talk' t' me no more."

Shit.

They pedalled on. "You aren't a vegetarian, are you?"

So he hadn't remembered the chicken burrito from her first night, the one she'd kept in his fridge. Or the chicken she picked up with the money he gave her the evening he passed out before she got back from the store. "No."

"Good. 'Cause these guys have the best beef dips anywhere." He turned into a quaint-looking house converted into a deli that served home-cooked food.

Tim ordered two beef dips, and two bottles of water, paid, and led the way to a table at the back with a view onto a garden. Uncommon in Florida, gardens, probably because the hurricanes blew them away, making people not want to bother with flowers, but the neighbouring building protected this one.

"Just so you know. This ain't a date," Tim clarified. "So don't go breakin' up with Emilio on my account."

"Right." Marcie nodded.

"I been thinkin' about what you said."

Marcie waited for him to say what specifically, because she'd said a lot of things.

"About practice relationships. I thought I could maybe try seein' what it's like t' at least eat dinner with someone. See if I could handle it."

"How is it so far?"

"We ain't got our food yet," Tim joked.

Marcie giggled. "That's why I like you. You're funny. I never laugh like this with Emilio."

"I don't know why you're with that little crook. And don't go blaming me."

"He was there." Marcie shrugged. "And he won't go away, even when something happens that should make him. Plus, I have a lot of time on my hands, you know, to spend it alone."

"Yeah. There's our food." Tim leapt up to go get it and set down two baskets.

Marcie took a bite when Tim did. "This is awesome," she agreed. And then didn't know what to say. So she kept eating. Tim ate too. Her phone rang. She shut it off. The only person she wanted to hear from was right here in front of her. But neither was talking.

Tim lit a cigarette after dinner. "You don't smoke, do ya?"

"No."

"See? We're not as much alike as you think. You wanna live with my habits?"

Live with? He was thinking about living with her? Marcie perked up with hope. "I've worked in bars all my life. My lungs are probably as bad as yours."

"You wanna have a three-second sex life?"

"I don't care. Just being near you makes me warm."

Tim shook his head. "You'd be better off with a blanket."

They giggled again.

"Even if we did get together, you and me would still be a dead end," he reminded her.

"Because you want kids."

"I know it might not work, but I want to try. And how would you like bein' with me, never knowing when it might over? You wanna get involved in something like that? You'd risk gettin' hurt and messin' up what you got goin' right now with your prize catch." Tim winked.

"In a minute. But get a sperm test before you leave me in case your pills have made you infertile. I wouldn't want us to break for up nothing."

"Yeah, the doc warned me about that. Plus, with all the booze and drugs? There's a risk the kid could be born with some kind of cancer."

"You like kids so much, you can babysit for Emilio. He left me with his yesterday." Marcie told Tim the story, which brought on more giggling. "So?" Marcie prompted when they stopped.

Tim hesitated. "I don't wanna make any commitments."

"You don't have to. One night and let's see."

Tim became lustfully quiet. "Okay. Ready?" Tim hopped off his stool and went and unlocked their bikes.

Without knowing if that meant *okay let's leave*, or if he was saying okay to spending the night, Marcie followed without asking him to clarify. She'd find out.

"You should get a light for that thing. It gets dark earlier now."

Marcie followed him back to Palm Grove in silence, where they dismounted their bikes to walk through the pedestrian gate, which Tim unlocked with his card. Since he didn't pause by her breezeway to say bye, she kept walking behind him to his.

At the bottom of his stairs, he asked, "You ever hear that song about this guy who said if he really loved a woman, he'd never phone her because he knew he'd only hurt her?"

"Yeah."

"I should be that guy. But I'm not." He kicked down his side stand and pressed her up against the wall with a hot, thin-lipped kiss, sending a flood of napalm through her body, leaving her barely able to stand. "I'm an ass." She hugged and kissed him back, letting her bike fall. "I'm guessin' you're comin' in."

They carried their bikes up the stairs, Tim unlocked his door, and the two of them walked in on Pat, stretched out on the couch with a beer.

Of all the stupid luck! "Here." She tossed Pat her keys. "Stay at my place tonight."

After Pat left, she and Tim collapsed in a giggling fit on the couch, where they necked more until he stiffened, swore, and relaxed. "See?"

He'd come?

"There's a football game on." He grinned boyishly. "You like football?"

"If I'm watching with you."

He stayed on top of her on the couch until he teased her at half-time, "You don't even know who's playing, do ya?"

"The red team and the blue team."

He playfully pushed her and got up for two bottles of water. Pat had left a bottle of rye and a half dozen beer. With a recovering addict.

"You want popcorn?" Tim offered.

"Sure."

When it was ready, he tossed pieces in front of Nubbles for her to chase. Could life get any better? Never before had she been so perfectly happy. "I could spend the rest of my life just like this," Marcie blurted.

"Yeah, well, don't get your hopes up or go burnin' any bridges. Tomorrow I could decide this was all a real bad idea."

But he turned off the TV and took her to bed, where he at least got his clothes off and entered her before coming this time. Then he went to the bathroom, probably to take his night pills, then crawled back into bed facing away from her.

The beginning or end?

His tossing, turning, and talking in his sleep kept her awake half the night. Was that normal?

In the morning, Tim's alarm woke her. After it buzzed a while, it also woke Tim. Hopefully, Pat wouldn't have left for work with her keys, meaning she'd be locked out. At least, she had his cell number in her phone and could call and ask to come pick them up.

The same angry man she'd woken up from his nap slammed the clock off and resentfully crossed the space from the bedroom to the bathroom without saying good morning. Did Tim even realize she was there?

After the shower ran and the toilet flushed, he emerged, shaven, and somewhat more his usual pill-propped-up self. "You still here?" he smirked. "I thought you'd ha' left."

She didn't ask, *Was that what you wanted?* in case he said yes. Instead she said, "I have a phone now," and wrote out her number. "Call when you want to get together again." Marcie grabbed her bike, checked for Nubbles, and bolted before she cried, because she could feel Tim would bail.

She knocked on her door and called, "Pat?"

"I was just gonna leave. How was your night?"

"Good."

"So am I going there or here after work?"

"Probably there. And what the hell are you doing bringing booze over to a recovering addict's place?"

"We drink in front of him all the time."

"But leaving it under his nose?"

Pat shrugged and left. Marcie wheeled her bike in, closed the door, then lay down on her mattress and openly bawled. She and Tim had had fun. Why would he want to throw that away? She loved how they laughed. Being silly. But the sources of their happiness were totally different. His was pills; hers, him. That was the inequality, the impossibility that made a bond between an addict and someone who wasn't one hopeless or make-believe. Life had proved too many times before that oil and water didn't mix, on anything more than a superficial level, for very long.

Not having slept all night, she drifted into a nap.

She jolted awake when she felt a presence standing over her. "Emilio! How'd you get in?"

"You left your door unlocked. What's the matter?"

"You scared me!"

"I mean, you bin cryin'. You look like a raccoon."

Marcie wiped under her eyes with her wrists, which came away all black from yesterday's eyeliner. "I was tired and didn't bother washing my face before bed."

"That's not what Pat said."

"Pat?"

"Yeah. You know. The guy you said could stay at your place last night 'cause you were sleeping over at Tim's. I saw him coming out of your place, where he wanted me to know he slept alone. So, was he lying?"

Either way she was dead. "No. I was at Tim's. We fell asleep watching football. I don't have a TV."

"I didn't peg you for a fan. And that's bullshit, or the three of you would have stayed there together. At least, by the looks of it, you got him out of your system. And, since you don't seem in the mood, I'll just be on my way. I'll lock myself out."

Feeling like death had passed over, Marcie showered. Still too shook up from Emilio's visit to eat, she sketched out some more ideas she hoped would convince Dennis to set the book in Florida and cycled to the copy place later in the afternoon to email him the drawings along with a storyline. Before leaving the copy store, she bought a photo album to put her art pictures in, and spent the rest of the day finishing *Conrad Crane*. Which meant she'd have to start searching for a publisher.

The next morning, her phone rang. A strange number was displayed on the screen. "Hello?" she answered neutrally, not even taking a guess at who it could be.

"We love the painting you did of our house."

"You do?"

"We'll come pick it up. The neighbours said they saw someone on a bicycle taking pictures a couple weeks back, so I'm guessing you don't have a car. Will you be home later this morning?"

"Yeah!"

The couple came, took the painting, and gave her two hundred dollars. *Yes!*

After they left, she cycled to the copy place to check if maybe the other two homeowners she'd sent pictures to had sent her an email. No. Still, one out of three, and it wasn't even Halloween yet. Not a bad start.

Later in the day, while she sat poolside, her phone rang again. The sun was too bright to read the screen, so she answered, hopeful it might be Tim calling, maybe to suggest doing something for Halloween, not knowing she'd made plans to attend a party with Emilio and family. "Hello?"

"I like how you've just taken over the whole book."

It was Dennis.

"That's not a kid's story! You've got the cat living in a shack with empty food dishes, no windows, laundry hanging in the yard, and a couple fighting in front of their kids."

"That's how some people here live. And why the cat leaves. He wants to seek something better."

"By smearing himself all over rich women?"

"He's a tomcat," Marcie reminded him.

"Opening their medicine cabinets and getting into their pills?"

"He's exploring his new environment and that's how quite a few Americans cope every day." Or, at least, one she knew.

"This is supposed to be a Canadian book. With Canadian content. For my Canadian publisher. I told you. I want *Tim* set at the Stampede. He rides broncs, chases the barrel racers, gets scared of the fireworks, tries dancing with the stage show performers."

"Right."

"And goes home again. A cat isn't going to want to go back to a home like you've portrayed," Dennis pointed out.

"Nor should he," Marcie agreed. "That's why he doesn't. Life isn't a circle. It's a progression. Did you read to the end?"

"Where, after Tim, or Tom as you've called him, gets bored hanging out drinking by the swimming pool and being waited on by the butler? So he runs away again, this time to a pool hall, to hook up with stray cats?"

"So he can feel like he belongs."

"How? As a pet, he had a home all his life."

"Well, he's learned self-reliance and he can't go back to being looked after. Not once he's had a taste of freedom. So the cats team up and grow to rely on each other for support. Do you want your daughters growing up believing they can run home every time they feel lost or scared, or that someone'll provide for them just 'cause they're cute?"

"Not when they're twenty, no. But this story's for kids, who should be home."

"Then why do you want to show them the glamour of running away?"

"What you neglected to depict was where the adventure goes sour, and my home wasn't a slum."

"Then why would the cat want to leave?"

"Curiosity about the big world! Not to escape."

"That was the theme of *Dodger*," Marcie reminded him.

"And it worked."

"You should stretch. Try something different."

"If it ain't broke . . ."

"Then it becomes formulaic. Okay, I can add a scene to show what can happen after too much drinking."

"I want you to redo the whole thing. For the average Canadian child, home is safe. Show that, since you want more freedom, show some fun adventures. And a turning point—something mildly disturbing that'll get the cat to go back to his family and be content there."

"Okay. Fine," Marcie conceded. Dennis was paying. So she'd try to sell her version to an American publisher located here.

"How are you?" he asked in a friendlier tone, having finished with business.

"Still wearing shorts." Marcie looked up at the sound of a siren, louder than when emergency vehicles simply passed on the highway, as they did every day and all night. An ambulance had turned down the lane.

"Holy shit, that's loud," Dennis commented.

"Yeah, I'm out by the pool. An ambulance stopped at the gate." Marcie wondered if the paramedics could open it and walked out to let them in. They waved their thanks, then stopped outside Tim's. "I gotta go. It's one of my neighbours." Marcie hung up on Dennis. Pat opened Tim's door to let in the medics. Not much later, they came down with Tim on the stretcher and loaded him into the ambulance. A very shaken up Pat followed them down the stairs. "Let me guess," Marcie accused.

"Fuck. I came home and found him passed out in a pool of piss and vomit."

"See? I told you you shouldn't have left booze at his place."

"It's a little late for blame now. And ever think you might have been the one to send him over the rails?"

Marcie's stomach went cold. "I accepted when he said he wasn't ready for a relationship." Not that she'd had any choice. "And left him alone. But the other night? He was the one who asked me to dinner. And he didn't even try to stop me from coming in. You were there. Did it look like I strong-armed him into spending the night?"

But obviously Pat had a point. She'd opened up emotions in Tim that he couldn't handle, which drove him to the bottle to quiet them. Imagine feeling all the time the same way Emilio's pulling out a gun made her feel. Which was what Tim had tried to explain and warned her might happen again; his body registered all emotions—happy or not—as extreme anxiety, to the point that oblivion was preferable. Once again, a pattern prevailed. It was a sad consolation; at least he'd had feelings for her.

"There goes his house again—if he even recovers." Pat shook his head.

"What do you mean?"

"Hospital bills."

"How long is he going to have to stay in?"

Pat shrugged. "Fuck, when I broke my ankle last year, I was in for a few hours, and that cost me sixty grand."

"You're kidding!"

"Doctors, hospital, X-rays—it adds up. At least my insurance paid half."

"Still. That's thirty thousand. How'd you pay?"

"I'm still paying. I give 'em a dollar a month and they can't touch me."

Marcie's mouth dropped. That might be an okay tactic for basic survival, but he probably couldn't qualify for a loan, like for a car, never mind a house, or pass anything he might manage to save on to his kids after he died, if he had any.

"Does Tim have insurance?"

"Doubt it. With his record? No insurance company in their right mind would touch him. Or offer him any premium he could afford. He's probably still payin' off his last rehab."

Marcie stood shocked at the damage she'd so inadvertently caused. As much as his ex, in far less time, and without much fun first. "Should we go see him?"

"He probably won't be conscious for a while, and when he is, I doubt he'll want to see either of us."

The tears flowed. Words or well wishes couldn't undo this harm both she and Pat were responsible for.

Pat retreated back into Tim's apartment; Marcie shuffled off home.

Emilio came by later when he dropped Abe off at the end of their work day. "You been cryin' again?"

"Tim's in the hospital."

"Drinkin' on pills again?"

"How many times has this happened?"

Emilio shrugged. "I've only seen it once before, but Abe said about ten. Life goes on. We still on for Halloween?"

"Yeah." Tim wouldn't be asking her to spend it with him now. And why spend the evening alone?

***

Mid-afternoon on Halloween day, Ken came by for his costume.

At six-thirty, after showering, Marcie stepped into a thong with scarves attached and hooked up a bra, also with scarves attached, as part of her Arabian princess costume. She fastened the bell belt and bell anklets, and slipped on the bracelets. After brushing back her hair and going extra heavy on the makeup, especially the eyeliner, she slipped on the headband veil and studied the effect in the mirror. Too bad she hadn't thought to buy fake nails to glue on. Her flip-flops would have to do as shoes. At 7:20, Emilio texted to meet him outside the gate, which implied he was running late and wouldn't have time to come in. At 7:29, Marcie went to stand in front of the office to wait.

At 7:35, she heard the approach of his car. As it got closer, Marcie noticed a woman in the front seat, who must be his wife. Penny had gotten the night off after all? Emilio had lied about her having to work? When he stopped, one of the kids opened the back door so Marcie could squeeze in with them, like a true friend of the family. No Canadian man would have kept his word if that meant taking his mistress and his wife to the same party; he would have either phoned with an excuse or not shown up.

"So, you're the children's book illustrator," Penny cooed in welcome.

"Yes."

"We've never had a famous person at our party."

And you still won't have had. Though maybe this was how people became famous, by allowing others to believe they'd achieved acclaim in another place, as they continued to pursue notoriety in a new locale.

"I'm Penny, Emilio's wife. I got somebody to cover my shift at the last minute so I could come. Carlos is going to love you! You'll be the hit of the party. Everybody there's got young kids, don't they, babe? You can give a little reading. Did you bring a book?"

"I didn't think to, no."

"Honey, did you bring ours?" Penny turned to Emilio. Not, *Cindy, could you please ask your father if he brought that book?* Penny behaved as if under the assumption that she and her husband enjoyed a true marriage.

"It might still be in the car," Emilio suggested, prompting the girls to find it in the back seat, as Emilio accelerated down the lane and turned onto the highway.

"Mom, can we open some of our Halloween candy?"

"No, dear. There's gonna be plenty of food there. And you'll be going trick-or-treating again. If we make it in one piece." She glared at Emilio, speeding too fast for her comfort. "Did you bring the camera?"

"Yes," Emilio snapped.

"Have you illustrated any other books?" Penny asked Marcie.

"I'm working on a couple right now."

"You're very talented. We have that painting you did of Emilio hanging in the hall. Everybody comments. You'll really fit in in New York."

"New York?"

"Where Carlos lives. Emilio's always doing something for somebody." Penny kissed Emilio's cheek. "Didn't he tell you?"

"No."

Silently, Emilio continued piloting the car down the highway. He exited into a residential area, turned onto a side road, then continued driving until they were surrounded by virtually uninhabited land. Eventually, the road led to a populated cul-de-sac. Emilio parked in front of one of the three large homes built around the half-circle of road. Penny brought the girls in; Emilio opened the trunk.

"What *the hell*?" Marcie demanded in a stage whisper.

"This wasn't supposed to happen," Emilio hissed back. "She didn't tell me till the last minute."

"That, and Carlos. I'm not moving to New York!"

"You're right. You're not. And don't even think about running off with my brother. Not even for one night or ten minutes!" Emilio shoved a foil-covered casserole dish at her to carry; he grabbed another one and led the way in. "By the way, you look great." He grabbed a handful of her ass.

Once near the door, Marcie pasted on her professional smile, as if she was headed into work, and placed her dish beside the other bowls and platters on the kitchen island. Already, the house was a circus. Kids screeched and ran. Music blasted. The adults, all holding glasses or cans, congregated in groups and chattered in Spanish. Emilio abandoned her, leaving her to stand alone like a gate crasher. A gorilla approached, eyed her up and down, and nodded. Frankenstein followed, carrying two beers, one of which he offered to her, before the bride of Frankenstein intercepted, dragging her man off.

Some men, not including Emilio, set up a poker game at the dining table, all while staring more at her costume than at what they were doing, making her wish she'd chosen something more conservative to wear. Penny ran up to her, toting Emilio in a King Louis costume behind her. "You changed," Marcie commented to Emilio.

"This is Carlos!" Penny corrected. "Emilio didn't tell you him and Carlos are twins?"

"No." Marcie smiled politely. Were they, really? Or was this actually Emilio posing as a fictitious brother to see if he could lure her into some kind of trap, like sleeping with him if he put the moves on her and offered her some kind of lavish New York lifestyle she couldn't refuse?

"Nice to meet you." Carlos bowed, speaking in an identical voice.

"Why don't the two of you go sit by the pool?" Penny practically shoved them outside.

"You heard the woman." Carlos grabbed two cans of soda, then once poolside, pulled together two plastic patio chairs, like the ones Marcie had in her living room, so they faced the pool.

"This is weird." Marcie stared at him.

"What?"

"I've never met identical twins before."

Carlos chuckled. "Fortunately, I don't have to deal with it much since Emilio left."

"He said he was from Puerto Rico."

"We all are. But we grew up in New York. The heat got a little hot for my worse half, so he left the gang and headed to Florida."

The gang. "What do you do in New York?"

"I build theatre sets."

"You must meet lots of actresses."

"A few."

"So why do you need, or why does Penny think you need, Emilio to set you up with somebody?"

Carlos shook his head. "The woman's blind. Or maybe she chooses to close her eyes. I dunno. Better than being a single mom, I guess."

"So, Emilio does this every holiday?"

"Basically."

"And the rest of his family knows? And doesn't rat him out to Penny?"

"And be responsible for an expensive divorce?"

"I guess that makes sense. But what a lying rat. He told me he's only been with five women."

Carlos guffawed.

"And he tried to give me the guilt trip over my history."

"So, what do you do for work?"

"I'm an artist. I used to work bars and restaurants, but I illustrated a children's book that went kind of big and . . ."

"Oh. So you're famous?"

"Not so much. Only one book's been published so far."

"I'd love to see it."

"Emilio has a copy. Penny wants me to give a reading tonight."

"Here's the perfect place. I'm the only one in this family who doesn't have kids. And they're all here."

A shadow loomed up from behind.

"Well, don't you two look cozy?" Emilio pulled up a third chair, dispelling any lingering suspicion that he and Carlos might be the same person, as a pack of screaming kids in costume ran onto the pool deck.

One of Emilio's girls tripped on her fairy wings and fell into the water. Marcie snatched her camera and snapped a picture. Another girl got pushed in from behind. When accused, the offender defended himself by saying he'd just turned around and she ran into him. "This is a push!" He demonstrated on another girl. Two girls then ganged up on the boy and shoved him in. His male allies exacted vengeance by wrestling the rest of the girls into the water. They retaliated by splashing the few dry boys on the deck until a man emerged from the house, yelling at Emilio in Spanish, pointing at the iridescent rainbows of face paint on the surface of the pool and the drowned deck. Penny also charged on scene, throwing in her Spanish two cents, and finishing off with, in English, "And you just sat there and did nothing!"

"I can't understand why the human race hasn't died out." Carlos shook his head. "And she thinks I should be married with kids of my own. Not a chance."

"Same," Marcie agreed.

"Maybe we should talk. You might like New York." Carlos winked.

Marcie watched Penny storm into the house and come out again with other mothers, towels, and changes of clothes.

"There goes their trick-or-treating," Marcie supposed, watching the kids being stripped out of sopping costumes in front of everybody. "And probably story time."

"And," Carlos smirked at his brother, "Emilio's whole day tomorrow. Eduardo's makin' him drain and scrub the pool."

"Like my girls started this," Emilio grumbled "It was his little brat who . . ."

"Monster Mash" suddenly blasted from the stereo at a volume louder than the songs before, cutting off the rest of Emilio's rant. The song, judging by the way everyone stormed the buffet, served as some sort of dinner bell.

"Shall we?" Carlos offered his elbow.

"Why not?" After picking up paper plates, Marcie casually inquired, "Say, do you carry a gun?"

"No. Nor do most Americans. I won't say only my brother does, but he's certainly in the minority. I'm guessing that he's still playing his intimidation games, since you asked."

Marcie nodded evasively. "Has he ever shot anyone?"

"That's something I've gone to great lengths not to know."

Which meant Emilio probably had.

After eating, for something to do, Marcie helped collect garbage and wash the serving dishes, then wandered off toward the sound of pool balls clinking together. "You play?" Carlos asked.

"Yes," she declared, so no one could blame her for playing well. But before a game could get started, Emilio poked his head in.

"We're leaving."

"Have a nice night," Carlos bid his twin brother goodbye.

"Don't be funny. Marcie's coming with us."

"I can drive her home."

"Hell you will."

Carlos grinned. "If you ever want to come to New York." Carlos slipped her his card. "I could get you in painting sets. Think of them as bigger illustrations. Literally, you could stretch your skills."

"We'd have to get married before I could work. I'm Canadian, eh?"

"That could be arranged."

If all else failed here? A man as attractive as Emilio but more on the up and up? New York didn't get as cold as Calgary, did it? And there were subways. She might be able to avoid being outside in the winter.

"Get in the car!" Emilio commanded.

She hugged Carlos goodbye and made her way out to the driveway, where Penny was hustling the girls into the back seat.

"So?" Penny prompted.

"Carlos is very nice." Marcie squeezed in beside the girls for the ride home.

When Emilio let her out at the gate, Marcie politely thanked him and Penny for the evening and said bye to the girls. After unlocking her apartment, she tucked away Carlos's card in her closet with her cash, just in case, then washed and undressed for bed.

5. November

Ken's monster costume floated face down in the pool when Marcie came out to paint late in the morning, having slept in, likely meaning Ken didn't win the contest, which meant he'd still be at Pat's, and Pat would be remaining at Tim's. Which worked out okay, because somebody had to feed Nubbles. Though had she not sent Pat—and, hence, Pat's alcohol—over to Tim's, Tim would be there looking after his cat himself instead of in the hospital.

Marcie stared at her sketchbook. She was really beginning to hate drawing what other people wanted, but that's where the bread was buttered. The sooner she finished and got Dennis's book over with, the sooner she could move on to what she wanted to paint, which was . . . what exactly, other than some interesting scenes she saw? What did she want to say with her art? She never thought art had to talk.

Marcie doodled a cat with a boy and his parents, all decked out in Western wear, all wearing happy smiles, at the Calgary Stampede. Next, the boy took the cat on the Ferris wheel, for which Marcie drew the cat's head sticking out of the boy's shirt at the top of the ride, looking terrified. Convinced the kid wanted to kill him, Tim— and Dennis could call him Tim now, for all she cared, because she'd never be seeing the real Tim again—then took off and hid in the bottom of a car on the toboggan ride—which no reader would see as a safe place of refuge, because every kid knew those taboggans went fast. On the next page, Marcie sketched a blur of passing taboggan cars, and on the page after that, Tim staggering off and throwing up. In an unreasonable attempt to make himself feel better, he consoled himself with corn dogs, candy floss, ice-cream bars, and mini doughnuts. Then, while still on a sugar high, he commandeered a bumper car and maniacally drove around slamming into everything.

At this point, Marcie started making notes, because the ideas were coming faster than she could draw. Tim could sit ringside at the rodeo and prowl the bull pens via the fence tops until a cowboy scooped him up out of harm's way and gave him a cigarette. He could down a beer next, before hopping onto the back of a bucking bronc. Rodeo clowns would rescue him from his wild ride, from which Tim would then pass out on his back. After recovering, he could watch the grandstand show from onstage, because no one would notice a small cat hiding in the wings, looking up dancers' skirts as they passed. He'd decide to dance with them until he got accidentally kicked. To nurse his internal injuries, he could hide under a barrel, which would be right next to the fireworks, where he'd be when they all got lit off. A stray spark could ignite his fur, which would be the last straw that would drive Tim home. The kid would find his naked cat on the porch the next morning and give it a bowl of warm milk, which Tim would turn up his pink nose at, having tasted the delights of beer. The last two pictures could be of Tim raiding the fridge for the kid's dad's beer at night, followed by him being found in the morning, passed out in a sea of empties on the kitchen floor. The End . . . of Tim's Stampede adventure, from which the cat returned home. Exactly what Dennis had asked for.

The following morning, again dressed quasi-conservatively, as on her book marketing trip, Marcie set out on her bike to visit some art galleries.

While the curator of the first gallery flipped through the pages of her portfolio, Marcie stared off at a corner of the ceiling, as if his decision didn't matter at all.

"You're talented. But they're too weird to sell. Sharks circling kids? Buyers want images on their walls that make them feel good, or something they can connect with. Or something that makes sense. Here you have a pool in a hotel room missing one wall with a sunset in the background . . . If you would have painted the sunset behind the pool outside, or finished the room as a room . . . Maybe if you do some ordinary beachscapes and homes without the Halloween paraphernalia, I could fix you up with a show, but these"—he shook his head—"are too disturbing."

"Did you see the birds?"

He nodded uncomfortably.

"They're ordinary," Marcie pointed out.

"They're not. They seem cute and playful at first glance. But their expressions . . ." The man shook his head again. "They look almost human. Evil, even. Like they're plotting something. My customers don't want challenging art."

"Thank you for looking." Marcie took back her photo album and left the gallery. Some success. Better than a flat-out *forget it.* Her work had at least gotten a reaction.

The gallery man gave her a card. "Take a look around. See what we feature. Then go paint something along similar lines and come back."

Gallery Two. "Interesting." The man nodded while flipping through the pages, then dismissively closed Marcie's album. "But we're booked solid for the next year."

The art world's version of *Don't call us.*

Gallery Three. "These are over-painted. Too much detail. You look at them from one angle or you look at them from another, and they're exactly the same. Take a look at *this* piece." This man walked her over to a wall on which hung a huge canvas of colour blobs. "Stand here." He paused, then moved to the opposite side. "Now come over here. See how it changes under the light?"

It did. The light washed out the lighter hues from one vantage point but not the other, causing the amoebas to appear just as ugly but in different tones.

"Plus, all your work is *of something*," he criticized. "Recognizable objects. Viewers want to use their imaginations. Work on some abstracts," he advised. "Something evocative, meaning just enough of something to evoke an entirety. I can tell you have a fine command of paint."

Marcie didn't take a card on her way out.

Gallery Four. "These are great! Sharks in the surf! Birds sliding down car windshields! How kitsch! But we deal in antique art. Try the tourist shops down by Channelside." Where Stan had told her to go. "These would make great mementos of Florida!"

Marcie got directions to Channelside and pedalled there.

"How big are these?" the gift-shop proprietor asked.

"The smallest one's about eighteen by twenty-four."

"Too big. I can only sell anything that fits into a suitcase. If you worked smaller, or on paper that could be rolled up in a tube . . ."

If, if, if! Marcie pasted on her fake tolerant smile. "I'll come back when I have something."

Another gallery wanted her website. Which she had, thanks to Stan. But she didn't know the web address off the top of her head. "But I have all the pictures right here!"

"That's the only way we look at new work."

Why? Marcie wanted to scream. That was like telling someone standing in the same room to call them on the phone! Stupid, but she took a card and said she could email her website address, which she'd do after getting somebody at the copy shop to help her upload her recent work, because she'd probably forgotten how.

At the place down the block, the owner sighed. "Photo-realistic renditions in surrealistic juxtapositions," he dismissed, tossing her album back at her. "It's been done."

Yeah, by Dali, and he had his own gallery. Maybe that was why. 'Cause nobody did it as well as he did.

Marcie left without saying goodbye.

At the next gallery, she heard, "You have a lot of technical skill, but my customers like flowers and nature. Impressionism. Light, happy colours."

"I have some herons by a duck pond," she said. He wanted nature.

"Yes, but"—the woman laughed nervously—"frankly, your birds give me the shivers. I feel like they're watching me. You should paint Halloween."

Marcie turned the pages to the Halloween homes.

"Ooooh. These would be perfect. Do some more and come back next summer so we can discuss an October show."

At the last place on her list, she was shut down before she even had a chance to share her portfolio. "No. We deal in estate collections, not with artists." Like somebody else had to prove the art was valid by owning it first. Like that song her father used to listen to: "You're Nobody Till Somebody Loves You." At this gallery, it was *you're nothing till you've been hung on somebody's wall.*

Her survival as an artist didn't look promising. If she had any hope, it would be through private sales. Or she could get married.

The tears started falling before she was out of the shop. At best, she'd be stuck illustrating children's books for the rest of her life, something her heart wasn't in. But even more likely, after a year, she'd end up having to go back to Canada and working at a regular job. If that was how it had to be, she was determined that it would be one where she could act normal, instead of like a laughing hyena, putting on some fake front to sell alcohol to customers. She shivered. She'd rather curl up and be homeless than go back to that phony servility. And *that* attitude scared her more. At least here in Florida, she'd seen at least one waitress over thirty. But, unmarried, she wouldn't even be able to work in bars here.

Unless Emilio and Joe let her work under the table in the strip club as a cocktail server . . . Was that better or worse than getting married? Worse. Because married to a bar owner, she'd see him far less.

Once home, she whipped her portfolio at the wall and threw herself on her air mattress to cry. Which she seemed to be doing a lot of lately. Because she wanted things to go one way and they always went another.

The morning brought a whole new perspective. If galleries said people wanted colour blobs and abstracts, fine. Without slaving over meticulous detail, she could paint faster. If she worked smaller—and or on paper—she could paint more rapidly still, and her supplies would be much cheaper. She wouldn't have to look at a subject she didn't like for as long and could move onto the next. Lifting only portions straight from nature or found scenes, she wouldn't have to worry about composition. She could do this, paint for the market tastes; that's what illustrators did. And, after yesterday, she'd acquired a pretty good idea what the market tastes were.

For the rest of the day, she walked around the property, photographing palm trees up close and from a distance. The duck pond could be made to appear different from different angles using iridescent paint. She could dab impressionistic scenes of the mall, which she'd already photographed half to death, in bright happy colours.

Late in the afternoon, to capture more reference pictures for sunsets, she risked life and limb by crossing all eight lanes of the Veterans Expressway at rush hour so she could get to the causeway by dusk, leaving her to cycle home in the pitch dark, unable to see more than one foot ahead of her. It was like living in Florida: taking one day at a time and unable to see ahead to where she was going. Unable to plan for or envision a future was unsettling. She'd spent her recent past picturing herself here, and now here she was, bumbling around in a dark unknown with many surprises.

Exhausted, as much from nerves as from cycling about thirty miles, Marcie ate and crashed. In the morning, she set up camp by the pool and painted about five different stages of a sunset in miniature, along with a garbage can on a beach, and a boat floating off the shore. Pictures of peace—something new to her, and a little challenging to take, after fourteen years of constant noise. Later in the day, she splurged on a ghetto blaster and some bargain-bin CDs so she wouldn't have to listen to silence.

***

"What'd you paint that for?" Emilio examined the garbage can when he came by in the morning. "Who'd want to buy a painting of trash?" Though he admitted, "It kinda looks good, the way the light's shining off it." *Success.* Exactly the effect she'd set out to achieve. A few more of those and she could go back to the gallery.

After Emilio left, she flipped through the pictures from the Halloween party: of the kids running on the deck in costume, shoving each other, and floating in rainbows of pool water. Perfect for her own cat book. Or a sequel! Having tasted independence at the Stampede, Tim splits and hitch-hikes to Florida. She'd cut Dennis in, even though he wouldn't have to do any of the writing.

Over the week, she put together a glamour collection by painting glossy close-ups of parts of fashionable bodies set against storefront backdrops, in arrangements she'd never seen done. The aquarium's gift shop might like some artistic renditions of sea creatures, so she banged off some of those, without getting too creative. She figured visitors would want accurate renditions, though she did combine several creatures and habitats, depicting what she hoped was the essence of the place.

While out for exercise on her bike, she stopped to send Dennis pictures of her progress so far. Already the copy shop was decorated for Christmas. She studied their greeting card collection. All traditional Santas, snow, snowmen, angels, wisemen, and Bethlehem. Nothing tropical. So she spent the evening coming up with some Christmas designs from the south, like sand Santas, elves in bikinis, a Christmas village of sandcastles and palm trees, banana leaf wreaths, sand snowmen, and green-and-red beach scenes teeming with seagulls in Santa hats and gold cockroaches.

Toward the end of November, she pedalled back to the copy shop, colour-copied her Christmas scenes onto cardstock, ordered business cards, purchased a giant box of envelopes and ribbon, then, once home, spent the evening folding cards in half, putting them together with envelopes, and tying them in packages of fifteen, one of each unique design—with a business card.

In the morning, she loaded everything into her bike basket and backpack, along with a sketchbook, pencils and chalk, and pedalled first to the aquarium, where the gift shop accepted the marine life paintings to sell on consignment, then back to the Channelside gift shop, which took everything Florida-themed, including the packaged Christmas cards.

"As a thank-you, can I do your portrait?" Marcie offered the same man who'd told her last month to paint smaller. "You won't have to sit still." She held up her camera.

"Sure." The man shrugged.

"I'll just sit outside, if that's okay." Because there, people could watch—potential customers who might want their portrait done. And, she couldn't get busted for conducting business without a licence on public property, because she'd be on private property, with the owner's authorization.

As she'd hoped, a small crowd soon gathered to watch. "Twenty dollars and I can do yours," she mentioned to everyone approaching near enough.

"Can you do my two girls?" A woman held out forty dollars. "Their grandparents'll love it. Maybe throw a palm tree in the background. We're from Minnesota."

Marcie happily abandoned her sketch of the gift shop proprietor and began her new commission, placing a few critical lines with light pencil, then shading in the shapes of the girls' faces with the chalk before detailing the eyes and lips with pencil crayons. The girls fidgeted before long, so Marcie snapped a picture and finished from that. Delighted with the result, the woman threw in a ten dollar tip. A few more people stepped up with their requests. Marcie took their pictures and sketched out their portraits.

By late afternoon, she'd pocketed almost half a month's rent. A few days of this every month and she could earn a livable income without marrying Joe. And it would give her the contact with people she was missing from not working, only under way better circumstances and for shorter periods of time.

As she stared at a docked cruise ship, another idea came to her for the ending of her version of *Tom*. After he fled the Halloween party because the kids wanted to paint his fur, he could stow away on a cruise ship and have adventures there. Then maybe get taken home by a nice family for a whole new start. The end as a beginning. The only problem was she'd never been aboard a cruise ship and didn't know what one looked like. So, she'd ask for a tour.

When the stores closed up shop and the tourists cleared out, she packed up her materials, locked her bike to a metal post, and mounted the stairs to the ship. No one stood at the top asking for boarding passes, so she photographed what Tom would see first. Keeping an eye out for some kind of ship official, she made her way toward the on-deck pool and photographed that, along with the straw-hut bar off to one side. She still hadn't attracted anyone's attention, so she made her way down a set of stairs, documenting her journey in digital.

After rounding a corner onto another deck with all kinds of stores, a man in a white uniform hurried in her direction. Uh-oh. Marcie rehearsed a speech to explain her presence, followed by an apology and a promise to leave right away, but the ship officer continued his haste, giving her a glance and a smiling nod. How easily she'd been mistaken for a passenger. She photographed him from behind, then made her way down some more stairs, which led to an empty hall of door handles and a maid's cart. The cabins. Walking with as much purpose as if she were on her way to her own cabin, she paused in front of an open door to the room a maid was cleaning to take a shot of its interior, including a porthole at the far end. After also grabbing a snap of the cart, where Tom could hide— maybe he could stay on board indefinitely, addicted to perpetual movement—Marcie followed more passageways and ended up at a discotheque, complete with disco ball, casting flickering jewels of light on the dark walls. Perfect for a cat to paw at. *Snap.*

Hearing the ship's whistle gave Marcie a sense of urgency that she should hurry and get off the boat. She climbed back up to the main deck and was greeted by a view of the sea. Her stomach panicked, while her mind reasoned she'd simply come up on the opposite side of the boat. Reassuringly, when she turned around, Channelside sat where it had been—only farther away.

Shit.

The gap of water between ship and dock would be nothing to swim, but a distance of about a hundred vertical feet separated her from the water. A gate barricaded the gap where the stairs had been. Stuck on the boat, she'd become an actual passenger. A stowaway. Life mimicking art. A criminal act. Worse than selling portraits without a permit. If caught, she could be sent back to Canada from the next port. Which was where? And how long would it take to get there? Was the boat even coming back or just moving on? She'd have to fly home with no passport; it was safely locked in her strong box at home. She closed her eyes and wanted to cry.

Not the thing to do if she didn't want to call attention to herself. On a cruise, people were happy. She dug deep for that old professional smile. A steel drum band played Caribbean music. The straw-hut bar featured milky blue umbrella drinks, advertised on a chalkboard as Bahama Mammas. The Bahamas was in the Caribbean. Maybe that was the ship's destination. Hopefully then it would come back and not continue on to, say, Europe. She couldn't ask; real passengers would know where they were headed. If she did, she'd be busted as an unpaid guest.

She sat on a deck chair to think. And noticed a hot-looking man by himself. He looked up and smiled. She smiled back and said, "Hi." He said hi back. He looked safe to ask. "I was wondering . . ." Marcie got up and sat closer to him.

He waited happily and expectantly for the *what.* She couldn't come out and blurt, *Do you know where the boat's going?* Especially not without further feeling him out. "Would you like your portrait done?" Marcie said instead. "For Free."

"Okay." He shrugged suspiciously.

Marcie took her sketchbook and pencils out of her pack and set up. While ostensibly assessing his proportions, she tried to see into his eyes—his character. Marcie mapped out some line angles. "In return, I'd like to ask you a question and you have to promise not to tell anyone that I asked, or that I'm here."

"Okay," he agreed again, curiosity piqued. "I guess."

"Where are we going?"

"We just met." He winked. "But I think this could go somewhere. You're cute."

In spite of her panic, Marcie laughed. She liked his relaxed sense of humour. "I mean the ship. Where's it headed?"

"The Bahamas."

"And then? Are we sailing someplace else or coming back here?"

"Back here." His expression changed; the subject now scrutinized the observer. Understandably. Because these questions were basic. Anyone on board should know.

"In how long?"

"Three or four days."

Marcie sighed with relief.

"You don't have a ticket, do you?"

"No."

"How'd you get on board?"

"I'm an artist." She passed him her business card. "I came on board to take photos for my next children's book, but there was nobody around to ask, so I gave myself a tour, and the ship left. Like what happened to my fictitious cat."

"Just pretend you're legit. The staff probably won't care. I don't know what the penalty is, but I wouldn't let any of the higher-ups find out. But no need to get all panicky either."

"As long as no one sees me sleeping on the deck."

"You can stay in my cabin, if you don't mind sharing my twin-size top bunk. One of the other groomsmen is sleeping on the one underneath. Bunch of us are here on a stag."

"Thank you! That'd be awesome."

"Just so you know who you'll be sleeping with, my name's Dwayne." He extended his hand and gave her his card.

"Marcie." She gave him hers.

"You Canadian?"

"The accent?"

"Yep. I thought so. We're from Chicago. We get more snow than you guys. Which was why we decided to take Jerry to the Bahamas—to get away from all that cold for a week."

"I couldn't take it anymore. Why I moved to Tampa."

"Don't you need a work permit or have to get married or something to stay in the States?"

"Or be a business, which is what I'm working on," she said, so Dwayne wouldn't worry that she'd be trying to manoeuvre him into proposing. Still, she didn't want to *discourage* him from trying if he was interested. He was nice looking, fit, and—she glanced at his card—a banker? "Though if it happens . . . you know, if I met someone . . . we could both move. Florida has banks."

"I'd be crazy not to consider it."

"So, why do you stay in Chicago if you hate cold and want to get away from it, when you can legally move someplace hot?"

"Sometimes I ask myself the same question. I was born in Chicago. So I have family there. They were all born there. The people are great and I have a good job, though, lately, believe me, I have been tempted to put in for a transfer. Minus eighty with the wind chill?" Dwayne shook his head.

"Do it."

"After meeting you, I just might." He grinned.

Marcie tried to control her soaring elation by focusing on the finishing touches on her portrait, adding the colour just right to capture the light reflections and shadows. "Ta-da!" She showed him.

"Holy shit! That's incredible." He gawked at the chalked version of himself. "I'm paying you for that." He handed her forty dollars. "Can you do the rest of the wedding party?"

"For sure!"

"Dedicated to helping small businesses, even on my vacation." Dwayne smiled in a parody of himself making a promotional bank advertisement.

"Is that what you do?"

"Yeah. I specialize in offering loans to small start-ups."

"So, where are the other guys?"

"The bar, probably." Dwayne studied her workmanship. "You said you illustrated a children's book?"

Marcie nodded.

"So are you, like, famous?"

"Working on it."

"With that kind of talent . . ." Dwayne showed his portrait to the guy on the chaise next to him. "Look at this. You should have yours done. Forty bucks."

"You can do one o' my kids. I'd pay you eighty bucks just to watch you try an' make 'em sit still."

Marcie showed him her camera.

"That's cheating. You got a card and a cell phone?" Dwayne's chaise neighbour asked.

"I do." Marcie handed him a card.

Dad pocketed it then went back to his book.

"Let's go find the guys." Dwayne took her hand.

They weren't in the bar but sitting on the edge of the upper deck with their feet dangling over the side, drinking beer. Dwayne introduced her then had them all turn around so she could photograph them as a group and individually.

"But no drawing now." Dwayne kissed her. "Let's go for a walk."

They strolled around every deck on the ship, pausing often to kiss and stare out into the ocean. When using the bathroom, Marcie texted Emilio, so he wouldn't freak out and call the cops once convinced she was missing: AM ON A BRUISE 4 3 DAXS.

"Let's get dressed for dinner," Dwayne said, when she came out. "Since it might take us a while." Dwayne hugged her to him as a hint of what would slow the preparation.

"I'll also have to buy dinner clothes."

"Right. Those are your only ones, aren't they?"

Dwayne walked her to the boutiques, then showed her where he'd be waiting. Marcie bought a dinner outfit, a couple changes of underwear, a sweater for the air conditioning, and a second pair of shorts and shirt to wear the next day while the other set hung to dry from a wash in the sink.

When she came back, Dwayne handed her several business cards and slips of paper with names on them. "I got you some customers."

Marcie spent the next day drawing their portraits while Dwayne hung out with his friends. One woman even offered to pay Marcie to watch her kids when they docked, "So I can spend some alone time with my husband on the island."

"I lost my passport," Marcie used as an excuse to explain why she'd be staying on board. Though how lost could something be on a ship? So she added, "I dropped it overboard." So the woman wouldn't enlist the whole crew to look.

"What a shame," the woman empathized. "Maybe on the way back, then."

"Maybe." On a cruise ship, there were at least things kids could do, unlike in a commercial area of Tampa.

After the boat had practically emptied onto the island, Marcie painted the wedding party, as a group and individually, and scooped more portrait work from some staff remaining on board. At the end of the day when everyone returned, Dwayne showed her pictures he'd taken of the island and said he'd send her some by email if she wanted. Then collected money from the guys to pay for their portraits and took her to bed early.

As the ship approached Tampa at the end of the third day, Dwayne held her. "You know. I hope you were serious, 'cause I'm putting in for a transfer to Florida."

"Really?" But would he actually? Or would life get in the way, even if he meant what he said now. Family demands, work, or he'd meet someone else and have second thoughts about ripping up his life for a shipboard romance and settling in a strange new city when he'd never left his home town for more than two weeks. Time would have to tell. One more thing to wait and see about. And that was starting to make her half-mental—never being able to anticipate what would happen tomorrow. She had nothing to lose but wasted energy if she couldn't stop herself from hoping too much for Dwayne to come through. She'd gotten to like him—a sober version of Tim. At least Dwayne's memories of her would be more positive. He'd have his portrait, and they'd shared a couple of days and nights of his vacation. Tim would forever associate her with another round of rehab and the loss of his hope of buying a house.

"Really," Dwayne assured her.

"By the end of February?" When her prepaid rent ran out.

"Maybe sooner."

Marcie grinned to hide her nagging doubt. Bankers didn't just uproot and marry waitresses, or artists, but she didn't want doubt sabotaging possibility. Eventually, things might change. Especially for famous artists.

"But you'll have to find us a place in whatever city the bank decides to send me to."

"Not a problem. If you can send me half of the rent." She wasn't completely stupid, signing a lease on some place she couldn't afford before she had any concrete proof of his commitment.

"We'll talk. You have my card?"

Marcie nodded. "And you have mine?"

"Yes. But if you don't hear from me right away, it'll just be because I'm busy with the wedding and Christmas and New Year's, and I have been known to lose things."

Regular guy stuff.

Together they walked down the steps toward her bike, where they kissed goodbye until his buddies hollered at him for the third time that their cab was waiting.

Marcie pedalled home. She no sooner had the key in her door when Emilio flew out of Jim's. "Where the fuck have you been?"

"I sent you a text before my phone died." It hadn't died, but it could have. Conceivably.

"What the hell's a forty-three-day bruise?"

"A cruise for three days," Marcie corrected.

"You didn't say anything about going on a cruise."

"It was sort of an accident. I went on board to take pictures for my cat book illustrations and the boat left port."

Emilio shook his head. "You fuck anybody?"

In response to his tone, she almost said no out of fear, but some suicidal impulse made her blurt, "So what if I did? Carlos said you bring a different woman to every family party and who knows how many more you have in between?"

"You believe him? He always tries to discredit me. You think I want to risk giving something to Penny?"

"Oh! And there's another lie, right there, because you told me you didn't have sex with your wife, just that you literally slept in the same bed."

"If you're gonna marry Joe, you can't be riskin' givin' nothin' t' him, neither," Emilio shifted the subject. "You wanna go meet him?"

"Now?"

"Why not? Have a shower. Change your clothes. Wear that camisole I gave ya."

Meeting Joe couldn't hurt. What if Dwayne didn't come through?

After showering, she threw on some jeans and the camisole as a shirt. And a sweater. The evenings were getting cool.

"Hot damn! Look at you!"

But instead of walking across the property, as she assumed they'd be doing, he led her to his car. "Where're we going?"

"I told you. Joe owns a strip club."

"I can't go out in public in underwear."

"Trust me. Most women there'll be wearing less than that. Got your camera?"

"Yeah, why?"

"You can probably get work from the strippers."

Like bar people ever paid money for art. When she had her art on display where she worked, guys often asked, *Why are you working here? You're so talented.* When she answered with, *Want to buy a painting?* they always said, *I can't afford it.* Even though one painting cost less than their average daily bar tab. *That's why I'm working here.* Then again, strippers weren't the usual bar people she'd had experience with, though, on Sundays, when bars had to close, industry people used to meet up and drink at strip clubs for somewhere to go, because strip joints, dumb as it sounded, could stay open, meaning to the religious, who made the rules in the first place, drinking and watching women get naked was more morally acceptable than drinking and hanging out with friends on Sundays. But Marcie had never met or talked to any of the strippers.

When they arrived at the club, a tall, bald, heavily muscled, tattooed man in a leather vest and jeans greeted them at the door. His gold earrings and chains flashed as bright as the two gold crowns on his front teeth; the rest gleamed shiny white. The man—Joe?—slapped Emilio on the shoulder then looked over at Marcie. His dilated pupils took up most of his eyes. High already. "This must be my future wife!" he exclaimed.

Marcie smiled back at this force of nature who could kill her simply by rolling over in bed. A man who could have any woman he wanted. And likely still would, officially married or not. Hopefully, the steroids would have shrunk his penis, or else it wasn't as proportionally large as the rest of him, otherwise he'd wreck her insides. Would Immigration even buy that a guy like this with his bad-boy, movie star–calibre looks could care about a cute but relatively plain non-US citizen enough to want to marry her? Better to hope Dwayne would come through. But already, he seemed so far away.

"Emilio was right. You are a sweet little thing." Joe pulled her close in a hug, nearly crushing her ribs.

Emilio wandered off to the bar, leaving the new couple to get acquainted. *So, how many men did you screw in jail?* It was the first question that popped into her head. She couldn't imagine any man forcing himself on Joe. If Emilio wanted to protect Penny—never mind that Marcie should want to protect herself—information about Joe's prison sex should be important to know. Yet how could she ask? Or trust he was telling the truth? Or believe that numbers meant anything? Just one could be the wrong one. Or multiple could all be clean. Though anything up the ass carried a risk . . . and the thought of him having been with another guy wasn't exactly a turn-on. With enough pull, could they buy women in prison? Enough drugs got smuggled in, that was for sure. Happy prisoners would make the guards' lives much easier . . .

"What do you want to drink?" Joe offered, leading the way to a table.

"A beer's good."

Joe got a beer out of the fridge and brought it to her.

"Stay put and look pretty. Emilio and I got some business to discuss."

Joe entered a door to a back room, where Emilio had already gone. The club hadn't opened yet. Marcie stared at the empty room filled only with tables, the stage, portable shower stalls, poles, lighting that wasn't turned on, and snapped a few pictures. Another place a cat could go.

Eventually, Emilio came out to toss her the keys to his car. "We're gonna be a while. Gimme your camera, so I can get some shots of the girls later."

Better he take them. Marcie handed over her camera, then drove herself home.

Mid-evening, Emilio called and told her to go over to Joe's. Then a voice that was Joe's told her, "I want you in my bed when I get home."

Marcie went. Easier to go than explain why she was hesitant.

At some point in the night, she heard feet on the stairs, a key in the lock, the opening of the door, then a booming voice announcing his very large presence. "This ain't gonna be no fake marriage," he promised, barging into the bedroom and hitting the light. "An' I'll prove it to any official who wants to watch us fuck." He grinned like a large child about to try a new toy. Marcie could only hope he cared about not breaking it.

Joe's touch felt good. Dwayne was two months away. Maybe. Did she want to put the rest of her life on hold till she knew? Or engender bad feelings in the place that she was?

Steroids hadn't made Joe small at all. And he hurt, even though he tried to be gentle. "You're big."

"You'll get used to it."

After how many times? And if she feared the pain, she wouldn't get turned on, and then it'd hurt worse. What if he wanted sex again when he woke up? Before she recovered? She slid out of bed and dressed.

"Hey, where're you goin'?"

"I'm sorry, I can't."

"That's too bad." Joe let her go.

And that was that.

In the morning, Emilio came by with her camera and drew her to him in a hug—his prelude to sex.

"I can't."

"Why not? Joe knows I ain't givin' you up."

"I'm sore," Marcie explained.

"Aw, shit." Emilio left, ticked.

She didn't tell him it wouldn't be happening again. Let him find out from Joe or just go away. Sex for the sake of itself was starting to lose its appeal. Whether or not she heard from Dwayne, when her rent ran out, she should move to another city anyway. Too much of her old life was repeating itself here. And she was beginning to feel very done with it.

Shaking her head half in disgust at what men wanted close-up shots of to look at, she scrolled through the pictures Emilio had taken with her camera . . . though why turn up her nose at a possible new market? Some of the contorted positions and aspects of female anatomy would be a challenge to paint, which she ended up spending the day doing, skipping her usual bike ride because she was too sore to sit on the seat.

6. December

The first of December dawned cooler, so Marcie painted inside in the morning instead of out on the lanai. The afternoon warmed up enough for the pool deck if she wore a sweater and sweatpants. Which she'd only brought one pair of. Maybe time to buy some of that winter wear she'd earlier laughed at. It was getting dark earlier now, too, plus the whole day had been overcast. The Florida winter was coming. It was the first day she hadn't seen sunshine.

After an early dinner, wearing her sweater and jeans, she decided to bike to the mall. Entering it felt like walking into the North Pole, and not just because of the air conditioning. The main hallway had become Santa's Village. Carols blasted over the loudspeakers. An actor dressed as Santa waved from an elaborate throne inside a cardboard castle covered in fake snow, surrounded by a flurry of wax elves frozen in various positions. Glittering snowflakes dangled from the high ceiling. Farther down, a team of incredibly real-looking reindeer, led by one with its nose painted red, were hitched up to a sleigh on fluffed fiberglass snow. In a relatively quiet corner of the mall, the characters from "The Twelve Days of Christmas" played out their parts as cast bronze sculptures! She'd seen enough of those around Calgary at Stampede time, of cowboys, horses, and bulls, to know what those bronze statues cost. Here, twelve giant lords leapt, eleven slightly smaller ladies danced, ten maids milked ten cows that were only slightly smaller than real cows, nine life-sized drummers drummed, eight swans "swam" in one of the fountains, seven pipers piped, six geese sat on some bronze eggs, four birds called beside three French hens, and two turtle doves snuggled under a cast-iron pear tree, in which a partridge sat. Five rings in bronze formed part of the archway leading into the whole exhibit.

Marcie rapped on a cow. Solid, not hollow. Whistling in disbelief at what the whole menagerie must have cost, she calculated her estimate on her phone. Fifty-nine life-sized figures, including the cows, multiplied by 3,000, which was what one of those cost in Canada, totalled $177,000.00. Add to that, the birds, say, at a quarter of the cost— another almost $20,000.00 for those. Plus, the pear tree and the five rings? Her guesstimate came to about $200,000.00 CAD, just for Christmas decorations in one small corner of the mall! Marcie's head swam like the swans. Add the inestimable expense of Santa's Village, the elaborate wreaths and ornaments hanging from the ceiling, and the cost of moving all the stuff out of and back into a storage facility large enough to accommodate the whole lot . . . stupefying. Imagine if the people eking out a living in their shacks and Quonset huts down by the airbase could see this. Then again, mall security probably wouldn't even let them in. Although, who would be able to tell the difference between the real poor and those who just dressed like they were poor, with popular fashion imitating ghetto style?

In contrast to the decorations, clothes here in Florida were so cheap. Her bill for two pairs of sweatpants, two hoodies, a couple of long-sleeved shirts, another pair of jeans, a light winter jacket, and socks but no gloves—the whole mall had run out—came in at just over one hundred dollars. Before fleeing the frigid air conditioning of this fabricated winter wonderland, she photographed everything, including one of the kiosks. Something she might consider renting next year, if not here, in another mall.

Over the next few days, Marcie designed more Christmas cards from her photos of the mall decorations, painted them, copied them onto cardstock, bought envelopes, packaged them, and cycled—wearing socks on her hands—back to all the places that had taken her other work on consignment. Some of her pieces had actually sold! She collected the money, promised more canvases, then capped off the day at Channelside, where most of her previous cards had been cleaned out. The shop owner was delighted to receive more, and even passed on some portrait commissions from people who'd seen the sketch she'd done of him, which he'd put on display! This whole gamble was working!

"Are you the artist?" a customer asked while she was there.

"Yes."

"Can you do me?"

Marcie looked to the proprietor, who nodded, giving her the go-ahead to paint inside his store, which was good, because outside, her hands would freeze numb.

While Marcie sketched and chalked, other people peeked in the window and came in, which led to a profitable evening. Before leaving, Marcie nabbed a cruise ship schedule so she'd know when a visit would yield the most customers. In the winter, cruise ships passed through more frequently.

Doing portraits at least gave her a chance to talk to people, even if just about where they were from. She learned about other parts of the States—and didn't have to listen to depressing confessions, like the ones she'd heard in the bar. *I just hit a pedestrian*, she'd once had a guy say to her. With the way his eyes had darted around nervously, he likely hadn't been making it up. *I didn't see her! She came out of nowhere! I need a drink.* Like more alcohol could make that problem go away. It was the cause in the first place for all alcoholics' problems.

You're not getting it here, Marcie had flatly refused him. And risk the cops coming in and finding her serving a homicide suspect? One more reason she'd wanted out of the business—so she wouldn't be held legally responsible for idiots, the way government regulations were headed. Instead of pinning the blame on the people who drank, politicians wanted to put it on bar staff.

Next day, she'd read in the paper that the guy had been arrested; the cops found him passed out behind the wheel while parked on a side street after Marcie had kicked him out.

While out and about the next day—the last decent one in the forecast—she came across a community college. Which might offer art classes. Which appealed to her more as a means to meet people and maybe make friends than an opportunity to learn more about painting, though picking up a few techniques couldn't hurt. She stopped in to inquire and registered for a six-week class starting in January. No green card required, the cost was dirt cheap, and it'd be over before her prepaid rent had run out. Though why bother making friends if she planned on moving? Still. Two months was a long time to get through and the portrait business might slump, like everything else, after Christmas.

Emilio was waiting for her when she came home. "You seen Joe lately?"

"No."

"Good."

"It's kind of off between us."

"Oh. Too bad." Emilio shrugged, like he couldn't care one way or the other.

Marcie showed him what she had painted of the strippers so far.

"They're gonna love these! What are you doing for Christmas?"

Not another family party! She struggled to think of an excuse for what she could be busy doing, but couldn't think of anything.

Before leaving Calgary, Marcie had imagined herself spending the 25th on the beach with a little Christmas tree stuck in the sand. But with this cold, rainy weather? Not likely. At night, ice formed on the puddles; everyone who'd warned her about how cold it got in Florida hadn't been completely lying. And even if she and Joe had hit it off, she'd likely still be spending Christmas alone, or staring at his sleeping body, because Joe would be tired. Like she'd always been. After a month of working seventy-hour weeks, serving at corporate breakfasts, lunches, after-work cocktail parties, quiet dinners, and dance bashes—where out-of-control employees drank on the company tab—she couldn't remember a Christmas not spent too exhausted to budge off the couch, except to pee and maybe turn the page of a book. And that was in Canada. How much more manic would the scene be here at an American strip club? Joe might even stay open on Christmas if he wanted more money. He could probably make a killing from lonely men and trapped dads nipping out for a quick drink and the sight of some flesh to get through the day of family overload.

She wondered what Dwayne would be doing. True to his warning, he hadn't called yet, though she could call him. Just to say Merry Christmas.

"I'll be in Puerto Rico," Emilio surprised her by saying, instead of inviting her somewhere she didn't want to go.

"Oh. Nice."

"Maybe one day I'll take you."

So he could use her as a cocaine mule?

After he left, she felt like taking a walk. A quick lap around the property for some air. Just like up north, she had to put on a coat.

On her way home, after giving it some thought, she stopped by Tim's to see Pat.

"Hey, stranger." Pat opened Tim's door when she knocked. "Watcha doin'?"

"Just out for a walk. When's Tim back, have you heard?"

"The beginning of January."

"I'm guessing Ken's still at your place?"

"Yep."

"Where're you gonna go when Tim comes home? 'Cause now you know you can't be drinking around him. Unless you're going to quit. And he might not want you here because of what happened last time."

"Yeah. I should. Quit drinking, I mean. But you're right, I gotta do something about Ken. 'Less you're gonna let me move in with you," Pat joked.

"Actually, that's what I came by to talk to you about."

"Seriously?"

"If you pay half my rent. Then you can give notice on your place and take over mine in March. Ken would then be management's problem to evict."

"Right. You're movin' in with Joe."

"That's kind of off."

"Probably smart. Then where're you gonna go in March?"

"Someplace cheaper." In another city, but Pat didn't need to know that, because word could magically get back to Emilio if she breathed one word to anyone.

"What's Emilio gonna say?"

"He has a car. He can drive."

"I mean about me livin' with you."

"You're not around during the day. And Emilio and I'll just be in the living room on my mattress instead of in my bedroom on my mattress."

Still, Pat looked concerned.

"He's not gonna think we could be sleeping together, right? Because . . ."

"I know. You don't want to get shot. Me either. I'll make sure he knows."

"That's sounding like a pretty good idea, actually, moving in with you. My mom and my aunt usually give me a few extra hundred bucks around Christmas, plus they're paying for my trip home, though my divorce lawyer is costing me plenty." Then Pat looked like he had an idea. "What are you doing for Christmas?"

"Not travelling up north. No matter who pays."

"No. Not that I wouldn't want you to come with me, but that wasn't what I was going to ask."

"Then what?"

"Wanna cat sit?"

"Sure, I'll feed Nubbles."

"Great!"

Pat brought her in and showed her the routine.

"You know, it's probably a good thing you're moving away. So Tim won't have to go on looking at you every day."

"Yeah, he mentioned he didn't like me living so close."

"You reminded him of his—"

"Yeah, I know. His ex-wife. I've heard it more than a few times."

"You guys were like a train wreck to each other."

Tears welled up in her eyes.

"He felt something, too, you know," Pat said.

"I know. Feelings for someone else." Marcie wiped at her eyes. Not a great compliment. "Which he wanted to drown. Which is dumb, because alcohol makes people more emotional, not less."

"Timing's everything, too. If you two had met before . . ."

"If." Stupid speculation. "I'm sad that he never recovered."

"Life takes its toll on everybody. None of us are what we started out as," Pat philosophized. "Hey, you'll meet somebody else."

Why tell him she had? He'd just ask her why she was crying, then. Anyway, she didn't know if she had, really, because Dwayne hadn't phoned yet, though he'd warned her he might not right away—and she'd drop Dwayne in a minute for Tim. How much effort and energy did a two-minute phone call to say hi take?

"If you get rid of Emilio," Pat added.

"Yeah, like you're one to talk. You aren't trying any harder to get rid of Ken."

"Yeah. We're a couple of cowards. Maybe we belong together."

"No," Marcie corrected.

"Okay, well, I'll book my flight and come by an' give you Tim's keys. And maybe you can help me move my furniture outta my place one night when Ken's at work."

On her short walk home, she heard sirens approach and watched an ambulance turn down the lane. Again. This time when the gate opened, the emergency vehicle backed up onto her own breezeway, which meant it had come for Jim, or possibly Abe, but Abe was young, drank less, slept more, and was not overweight. Two paramedics hopped out and grabbed a stretcher out of the back. Abe ran out of Jim's, practically dancing in panic. The uniformed men entered Jim's suite. Marcie slipped past into hers and watched out the peephole until the ambulance left with Jim.

She ran out to ask Abe what had happened before he could go back inside. "Is Jim okay?"

"I didn't know he was diabetic. I thought he was just passed out. But when he threw up blood"—Abe pointed to a pool of vomit inside, which pretty much blended in with the shag carpet—"I called nine-one-one. Turned out he wasn't supposed to be drinking at all. That bracelet he wears?" Abe shook his head. "You want to come in for a drink? I could use one."

"No, it's okay." She'd throw up if she smelled somebody else's and didn't want to be roped into helping clean it up.

"Fuck. What if he dies?"

"I don't know." Marcie had never had someone die on her before, except her mother, but her father had taken care of that. He hadn't even bothered to tell Marcie her mother had died, until Marcie asked when she could go back and visit again at the hospital. "Does he have any relatives?"

Abe shrugged.

"Maybe he'll get a Christmas card with a return address. Or go see him at the hospital and ask him when he wakes up. I can go with you if you want. Maybe tomorrow, once he's admitted and might be conscious."

"Yeah." Abe closed the door in a daze.

Another alcohol casualty. What the hell was wrong with this country?

Emilio came by in the morning. "Abe tell you about Jim?" Marcie asked.

"Penny told me. Liver failure."

227

After they had sex, Emilio left to get Abe, but came back. "He's not answering. Feel like driving today?" He dangled his car keys from his hand.

No, she did not want to do Abe's job and be involved in whatever they did, but what excuse could she give? "I signed up for an art class," she blurted. The absolute truth. It just didn't start until January and had nothing to do with what she'd be doing today, but Emilio couldn't know that.

He nodded. "Maybe I'll take the day off work."

Which meant she'd have to hope Emilio didn't offer to drive her to said art class, and then spend the next few hours out. Or, she could hide in the closet. Which was where she spent the bulk of the day painting strippers anyway. Had it not been raining—a legitimate excuse not to bike— she would have hidden her bike in the bathroom so Emilio wouldn't see it if he checked up on her.

She was too paranoid.

For exercise, she did sets of push-ups, because, having hypothetically been out all day, she shouldn't feel like doing more exercise once she got home, nor did she feel like going outside in the cold rain.

Later in the evening, her furnace came on. The sky looked like snow was on its way. Which reminded her, Christmas was coming. Emilio would probably give her a gift before he left for Puerto Rico. Or bring her something when he got back. What could she get him? Maybe a wallet, something for all his rolled-up loose bills, though if he wanted one, he would have bought one already, and so many bills might not fit. But so what if he couldn't use what she gave him or if he didn't like it? It was better than not giving him anything. Who knew? Maybe she'd find something else to get him if she looked around.

While trolling the mall the next day for a gift, she found a white-gold money clip at a kiosk, telling her that more men than just Emilio and Jim disliked carrying wallets. She used one of Emilio's questionable hundreds to buy one of the larger clips, then sat on a bench to people-watch. Everyone's clothes had logos on them. People had become walking advertisements. Customers paid for the privilege of promoting brand names, something companies used to have to pay to have happen.

Which gave her an idea. She could promote *Dodger the Dog* the same way! If she bought T-shirts and painted the dog on them, along with the title of the book, she could sell the shirts and have the buyers pay to promote her book! She could send shirts to the publisher to distribute along with the books, though she was too late to cash in on this Christmas. She decided that for now, she would paint up some clothes and walk around with a few books to hand out to see if the idea worked. By the time her and Dennis's versions of *Tom/Tim the Tomcat* came out, there could be a whole marketing system in place, like there was for those syndicated Japanese cartoons.

Excited, she charged into a kids' store and bought little T-shirts, which she worked on painting over the following few days.

The next time Emilio came over, as she expected, he handed her a small wrapped package. "Merry Christmas, baby girl."

"Thank you!" Slowly, Marcie tore at the paper and tape, revealing a velvety box. She lifted the hinged lid. Diamond earrings—or fake ones in a good box—glittered from the silk lining. "They're gorgeous." Reverently, she tried pulling the backs from the posts, but couldn't.

"You have to unscrew them."

Which had to mean the diamonds were real.

"Go put 'em in."

Needing a mirror, Marcie ran off to look in the bathroom's. These were stunners, glinting blue and green sparks, and almost quarter karats. Not cheap. Marcie felt very in debt, no matter how he'd come by them.

"Let's see." He beamed proudly.

Marcie stood and let him look at her ears. Then announced, "I got something for you too." Almost embarrassed, she handed him her box.

"Hey!" he exclaimed with delight as he opened it. Having three kids, he'd likely had years of practice feigning joy. He tried to clip his cash with the clip, though only a portion of the bills fit.

"The strippers are done." Marcie pointed to the canvases.

"They're gonna love these." He held each one up to the light, then loaded them all into the car.

Marcie followed. "How's Jim?"

"Penny said he'll be home in a couple days. You should go see him. He'd like the company." So Emilio was okay with her having friends; hopefully he'd feel the same way about Pat.

Over the next week, she put the finishing touches on *Tim the Tomcat at the Stampede,* which she emailed to Dennis and snail-mailed him and his family one of her original, sunny Christmas cards, even though the weather now was anything but tropical. Tampa felt too much like being in Calgary: going to the mall, people drinking, busy roads and lots of cars. There wasn't even a beach in the city. But, she wouldn't be staying here, and where she went next would have a beach, which faced the real ocean and not just the Gulf, like Florida's west side. She'd go to the east coast of the State. Sit on the beach all day and paint portraits. Take up surfing. Meet surfers. Her consolation prize if Dwayne didn't come through.

She took out Dwayne's card, debating whether to email him or not. If she did and he didn't respond, that would put an end to the dream, and was she ready to give it up yet by initiating contact? Already, the possibility had stopped feeling real. She could snail-mail him a card. No. Because she only had his address at the bank. He might not actually receive the card, or his coworkers could get to it first, which could get him in trouble if he had a girlfriend. His email was his work address, too. What if it wasn't private? She should just call him. Both his cell and office number were on his card.

It would only be noon in Chicago; she'd wait until after work but before dinner, in case he spent his evenings with someone.

In the evening, just as she was about to call, Pat phoned. "Ken's at work," he said. Which meant it was time to schlep furniture.

Before going over to Pat's, Marcie, with Pat's help, moved her things out of her bedroom and into the dining room. "What's this?" Pat discovered the painting of Tim.

"Oh. I'll take it over to Tim's." Let Tim throw it out, which he'd likely do, since it'd be a bitter reminder to him of himself in the last of his better days. And he couldn't get much madder at her than he probably already was, and she wouldn't be anywhere near him when he erupted.

By ten o'clock, all Pat's stuff was in her place, leaving Ken only his clothes and a blanket, and Marcie no space to move. While Pat set up a man cave in what used to be her room, Marcie converted the dining room into her sleeping area, using one of Pat's dressers, not only for her clothes, since she'd lost the closet, but as a privacy divider. She set up her painting area by the patio door and on half of Pat's dining room table, and put her plastic patio table and chairs out on the patio. Marcie's mostly empty kitchen cupboards had become suddenly full. Pat's shaving paraphernalia and towels were stacked on top of the washer-dryer in the bathroom.

"You can put up the Christmas tree if you want," he said. Which currently sat in a box by her bike. "Watch TV, too, while I'm gone . . . or when I'm here." He grinned, because the TV was in his room. One of those jokes he'd be happy if she took seriously. "You hungry?"

"Starved. But I'm too tired to eat. Go ahead if you want. Once I'm in bed, I won't hear a thing." She didn't think. When was the last time she'd lived with someone?

Pat ordered in takeout and sat down at the table to wait for it to arrive. "This is nice, living with someone again. You know, just sharing space, being in the same room."

Maybe for him. For her, if she wasn't in love with someone, another person and his junk would be a test of her patience.

"If we get along, as soon as my divorce comes through, I'll marry you. Even if we just lived as good friends. I know it's crowded in here, but we could find a bigger place."

"If we got married, that'd make me responsible for half your hospital bill." Or all of it, if something happened to Pat.

"Yeah, but . . ." Pat shrugged, like a debt of tens of thousands of dollars on which he paid a dollar a month was nothing. "Then you'll never marry anybody."

Something she hadn't thought about before. Although, Dwayne should have good insurance and didn't seem accident-prone. Nor did he drink nearly as much as the guys around here.

"What if something happens to you?" Pat posed.

Since she'd never been in the hospital, that wasn't really something she thought of, either. "I'll deal with it if it happens." Marcie went to brush her teeth.

When she finished, Pat was paying the delivery guy for his pizza.

At some point in the night, loud banging on her front door and an angry voice shouting, "You motherfucker!" jolted her wide awake.

Pat stormed out of his room and hollered back through the closed door, "You had almost three months of free rent, so what are you complaining about? Buy your own fucking bed. And just so you know, you've got till the end of the month on my dime before you have to be outta there or start paying. I gave my notice on my place at the office."

Ken kicked the door in frustration.

"You want us to call the cops?" Pat threatened.

Silence answered.

"Bastard," Pat muttered. "Like I'll get back to sleep now, and I have to be at the airport by five."

"At least you can sleep on the plane," Marcie pointed out. And she could sleep half the day. Unlike dogs, cats didn't have to be let out on a schedule. Nubbles could use the litter box and wouldn't starve to death waiting a few extra hours for Marcie. "But, while I'm awake"—she threw on her sweats—"I better go cut you a key so you can get in if I'm not home when you get back." The discount store was open twenty-four hours.

Marcie woke close to noon, after a sleep so sound, she hadn't heard Pat leave. Before starting her own day, she grabbed the painting of Tim and walked over to feed his cat. Feeling like an intruder, she opened the door only a crack at first so Nubbles wouldn't bolt out. Weird being there all alone, in what she'd once hoped could be her home. With Tim. After finding no free nail in a wall, she opened the closet and propped the painting up against his clothes—the only place she could think to put it where Nubbles wouldn't be able to shred it with his claws. She then cleaned the litter box, put out fresh food and water, played with Nubbles a bit, then went home and put up Pat's Christmas tree.

After painting till mid-afternoon, she bundled up and walked, rather than cycled—since it was raining—to get a coffee. Dwayne would be seriously freezing up in Chicago. Christmas offered an excuse to call him, without coming off like a deluded fool or seeming like she was pouring on pressure. Talking to him would either set the plan of living together in motion or kill it, and she was getting to the point where she wanted to know whether he'd been serious about a transfer to Florida or not, instead of letting herself go on dreaming. She wanted some definite clue about what was next, when her rent ran out in February. She knew she'd be leaving Tampa; and, unless she wanted to live out of a rental car for a month, she'd have to start poking around on the computer for an apartment some place. Though maybe being a temporary transient could be fun; she could explore new horizons in person before deciding where she might want to put down roots.

Marcie took out her phone and keyed in Dwayne's number. Not surprisingly, his phone went to voicemail. At least she knew that it was him, and that he hadn't been pretending to be somebody else. "Hi Dwayne. It's Marcie." She tried to keep her voice light. "From the cruise. Just thought I'd call and say merry Christmas."

When her ass started to hurt from sitting on the coffee shop's hard, wooden chair, and she'd finished her latte, she ripped a couple of advertisements she wanted to paint out of the shop's magazines and headed for home. In Calgary, she would have killed for such peace, leisure, and physical energy all at the same time. Now, the boredom was killing her. Or not so much boredom, but loneliness. She wanted to be with someone, but not just anyone. Someone who excited her like Tim and Dwayne had. Emilio had been a why-not because he'd been there, but she didn't know how to get out of that now. But even he was away for the holidays. Tim, Pat, Joe, Jim, and Ken all weren't home. Abe she'd never had much to do with. Well, the holidays would be over soon, so there'd be portraits and art class. The weather would warm up again and she could ride her bike again. In two months, she'd leave Tampa . . . and then what? She'd start the relocation process all over again, likely alone, because that was her life. No man she wanted ever came through for her.

When she passed Jim's place, she noticed the lights were on. Which didn't mean Jim was home from the hospital, necessarily; Abe could be there. Nevertheless, after using her bathroom and ditching her umbrella, she knocked on Jim's door. Jim opened it a crack and peered out suspiciously, then, when he realized who it was, broke into a grin. "Hey!"

"How are you? I saw your lights and thought I'd stop by. See if you're okay. If you need anything."

"Yeah, thanks, though if I did, I'm supposed to move my own lazy ass to go get it. Doc says I gotta get exercise."

"Hmmm." Marcie nodded in empathy.

"And, worse, no more drinking," Jim continued. "Ever." He shook his head at the impossibility. "Hey, you wanna go for a walk? Might help take my mind off not drinking!"

More walking, and in the cold rain, was the last thing she wanted to do, but . . . "Sure. I'll grab my umbrella." And a card. She scribbled a *Get well* and *Merry Christmas* message on one of her sand Santas and handed it to Jim before leaving.

"Thanks. My only Christmas card."

"Not even from your mom?"

"She'll phone on Christmas." Jim stood the card up on the coffee table before closing the door behind them and putting up the hood on his waterproof jacket.

After half an hour of walking, Jim asked, "Hey, while we're out, wanna grab dinner?"

While waiting in line to be seated at the Mexican joint, a place that brought back memories of Tim, Marcie's phone rang. *Dwayne!* Without thinking of possible repercussions, she answered.

"I'm glad you called!!" he exclaimed, without even making excuses for the long wait. He had warned her he might not phone for a while, and she always tried to play the good sport. "How are you?"

"Good! You?"

"I put in for that transfer to Florida."

"You did?" Was he lying?

"To Orlando."

"Oh!" So what if it was landlocked? They could drive to the ocean. "When will you hear?"

"I don't know. But I'll let you know as soon as I do."

"If it doesn't work out, Florida has lots of banks. You could just apply at one."

"I could. How's the weather?"

"Right now, cold and raining. But I'm told winter only lasts about six weeks."

"Beats the hell out of here. Right now it's minus thirty and I had to shovel my car out."

"Ugh." Marcie sided with him on the horror of it. A climate she never wanted to live in again.

"Okay, I gotta drive to my mom's. Talk soon," Dwayne signed off.

Grinning euphorically, Marcie hit the End key before her face fell; she'd spoken enthusiastically to another man while standing next to a living, breathing, gossipmonger, whose roommate worked for Emilio. Every word of that conversation, or at least its gist, would get back to her for-now and for-here boyfriend. She might have to bump up her exit date.

But really, what had she said? She replayed her words. Could Jim have heard Dwayne's? "A friend from Calgary," she brushed off, before Jim could ask.

But, nose buried in the menu, probably stewing over the fact that there was nothing on it that he wanted to eat, which the doctor would allow, Jim seemed not to hear or care whom Marcie had talked to.

On Christmas morning, after she fed Nubbles around noon, Joe phoned! "Merry Christmas!"

"To you too."

"Hey, doing anything?"

"No."

"Why don't you come over? I got some money for you. The strippers all loved their paintings. And, I thought, maybe we could spend the rest of day together."

Why not? "Sure. See you in a bit."

"Merry Christmas." He greeted her with a tired hug and a friend kiss when he opened the door. He looked as exhausted as she used to feel every season, and reeked of beer and cigarettes—the smell of a bar. "You wanna go for a drive?"

"Sure."

"First I need to wake up." He opened the battery compartment of his ghetto blaster and cut two lines of coke on the coffee table. Marcie declined, so Joe snorted them both, then more energetically led the way to his truck.

He drove along the causeway beside the placid beach, telling her stories from when he'd been in the Marines and how he'd ended up making enough cash smuggling drugs while in Panama, protecting the canal from local uprisings, to buy the strip club. Once discharged and back in Tampa, he continued his illegal trade, got busted, and did time in jail, but the others kept things going till he got out.

Instead of saying, *And you're still going to continue?* Marcie just nodded.

Joe parked at a beach. They got out of the truck and sat shoulder to shoulder on sand protected from yesterday's rain by a tree, staring out at the water.

"So, when's our wedding? You make me feel so at peace."

"I . . . I can't. You're too big." She tried offering him a compliment as a means out.

"We don't have to fuck."

He probably had enough other women for that. And being together might make him feel tranquil, but it made her incredibly nervous. And not just because of the thought that she could be arrested if she happened to be anywhere near Joe if he was busted by the cops again; his presence itself was unnerving. He just looked dangerous. And with him around, she'd never be able to ditch Emilio.

"Let me think about it," she hedged, too afraid to come right out and say no.

Joe shrugged and took on an air of disinterest, which made starting any kind of conversation impossible, which put her on pins and needles—an all-too familiar feeling as she'd spent most of her childhood on those. But she could tell he knew what the answer was. "Let's go." He started back for the truck.

"Thanks for the drive," Marcie said when he let her off at her place. "Merry Christmas." She waved, closing the door, glad that was over—and happy to be $1500.00 in small bills richer.

Before getting comfortable at home, Marcie went over to Tim's to feed Nubbles and noticed a light on. Since she didn't remember turning one on this morning, did that mean Tim was home? To make sure, so she wouldn't make the wrong assumption and let his cat starve, she knocked.

Tim's pleasant, expectant face clouded in anger when he saw her at the door. "What the fuck?"

"I wanted to make sure you were home and that I didn't just leave the light on from when I was there earlier."

"Where's Pat?"

"New Hampshire. And you won't have to worry about him moving back in with you—he's rooming with me.

So, since you're home . . ." Marcie held out Tim's key. He took it. "Okay, well, merry Christmas. And I'm sorry if I had anything to do with . . ." Her eyes teared up and she ran down the stairs.

The next time she took out her trash, just as she half expected, she saw the canvas of happy Tim lying on top of the dumpster.

7. January

The morning of New Year's Day, Marcie woke to a thundering roar overhead. She grabbed a robe and ran outside but saw nothing except Jim in a football jersey. "What was that?"

"The Bucs are playin' the Navy," Jim explained, which explained nothing.

"I meant the noise."

"Yeah." Jim pointed to three dots in the distant sky. The configuration circled around and shaped into fighter planes, which, with their dazzling lights bright as suns, approached at a concerningly low altitude, waggled their wings over the nearby stadium, and continued low above Palm Grove at a speed so slow, they seemed on the verge of dropping out of the air. The same deafening roar of thunder accompanied these military planes, casting shadows as they pulled up and headed south back to the airbase. Marcie stared up with her mouth open. "Wanna come?" Jim invited.

"Where?"

"To the game!"

Too much of an all-American experience to turn down: football on New Year's Day. "Yeah. Just let me get dressed."

"Hurry up. I don't want to miss the kick-off."

On her way in, Marcie plucked the beer out of Jim's hand. "You're not supposed to be drinking." Not that anything she said or did would stop him. He could easily run inside for another beer, and there'd be plenty for sale at the game. She thought maybe a little concern might make him more likely to self-police. If he couldn't? "You want to end up back in the hospital?"

Pat came back at the start of the week, looking worse than when he left. Not hard to figure out why. Family at Christmas, for most people, spelled too much food and booze.

By the end of the week, the temperature had warmed up enough to wear shorts again. Marcie grabbed her bike and cycled around to the stores she'd left Christmas cards at to collect unsold inventory and money from sales. Which was what she was out doing when Emilio, fresh back from Puerto Rico, called to arrange to meet her at home in an hour.

"Can't wait!" he signed off, before she remembered to warn him about Pat.

As Marcie neared home, she heard and saw Emilio's car turn down the lane. By the time she got to the gate, he was already inside the property, pointing a gun at someone who'd been trying to see inside her window and now stood with his hands in the air! She pedalled on scene in disbelief. "*Dennis?* What the fuck?"

"You know this guy?" Emilio lowered the gun.

"He's the children's book author!"

"What the fuck's he doing staring in your window? You didn't tell me he was coming!"

"I didn't know!"

"I thought I'd surprise you!" Dennis explained.

"Usually people knock on the door!" Emilio lowered his gun.

"I did. But nobody answered. Then, when I saw all the furniture and men's clothes all over the bedroom, I wasn't sure I had the right place."

"What furniture?" Emilio questioned. "A plastic patio table? You Canadians call that furniture?"

"Pat moved in," Marcie explained.

"Pat?" Emilio repeated.

"With his furniture."

"You didn't tell me that either!"

"I forgot. Besides, he's always at work when you come over, so I didn't think it would matter."

"She didn't tell me she was living with anyone either," Dennis mentioned in support, lowering one hand to wipe the sweat off his forehead. "Fuck. I didn't know Americans hated surprises so much, or I would have called first." He slumped back against the side of the building. "I could have had a fucking heart attack."

"You Canadians get so freaked out about guns. It's not like I shot it." Emilio shook his head and dropped his gun in his pocket.

"How was I supposed to know you weren't going to actually shoot?" Dennis turned to Marcie. "Who is this little . . .?" Dennis fumbled for an adjective for Emilio.

"Dennis, Emilio. Emilio, Dennis," she said in introduction, though a name probably wasn't what Dennis was after.

Emilio nodded; Dennis continued to glare.

Marcie's phone broke the silence: a call from a number and area code she didn't recognize. "Hello?"

"Marcie! How are you?" a vaguely familiar man's voice spoke in her ear.

"Fine."

"It's Stan. Remember me? From Clearwater."

"Yes! How are you?" *Why did he have to call her now?*

"Hey, I'm on the east coast on business in Fort Lauderdale and was wondering if you wanted to join me. Rent a car. See more of the country. When I finish, I thought maybe we could drive down to Miami and through the Keys."

"Sounds great! Can I call you back?"

"Sure."

"Who was that?" Emilio demanded.

"A retailer." It popped into her head, since she'd been seeing retailers all afternoon. "He's opening a shop on the east coast," she said, in case Emilio heard any key words, "and wants to talk to me about displaying some work there."

Emilio shook his head. "I gotta go pick up the girls. How long's your friend gonna be here?"

"I dunno. Ask him."

"Originally, I'd thought a week," Dennis said. Which implied he'd now be leaving sooner.

"Let me know when he's gone." Emilio got in his car, pulled a U-ie in the parking lot, and drove back out the gate.

"What are you doing with that little shit-scum?" Dennis, full of adrenalin, if not bullets, madly gesticulated. "Aside from thinking I was going to be shot, do you know what's almost as bad?" Dennis didn't pause to let her guess, but continued, "I don't hear any sirens! Which means nobody's called the cops! So a guy can go around, waving a gun, and nobody does anything?"

"I don't know if you *can*. Legally. People are just probably at work and didn't see anything."

Dennis shook his head and picked up his suitcase. "I need a drink! Got anything?"

"Pat probably has beer." Marcie unlocked her door.

Dennis set down his bag and walked toward the fridge. "So Pat is . . .?"

"A neighbour. Who's having problems with another neighbour who won't leave his apartment, so he moved in here."

"Is he going to shoot me?" Dennis snapped the tab on a can.

"No, we're just friends. And I'll replace the beer. So, how'd you get away?"

"Julie's mom's sick. She took the kids and went up to Edmonton for a couple days." Dennis took a swig of his beer and looked around.

"Yeah, I know. There's no space."

"How can you stand living like this?"

"It's only been a week and won't be for much longer. I'm not staying in Tampa. For obvious reasons. But don't say anything to anybody—nobody here knows I'm leaving." And now that Stan had called, she'd be leaving even sooner.

Dennis pantomimed zipping his lips. He guzzled more beer, then got down to business. "About those drawings."

"You don't like them." Marcie could tell by his tone. "I did what you wanted."

"To the letter. But the spirit's all wrong. The cat's still . . . corrupted."

"You don't leave home and stay innocent."

"Around here, I guess not. But for one, my audience is Canadian kids, and two, kids' books aren't about reality anyway."

"They should be. Then you might not get so many naïve kids thinking the world's all rosy and everything will turn out all right in the end."

"If you make kids afraid of life, they might not leave home," Dennis said.

"They're starting not to anyway because of high rent and real estate prices."

"*Tom* is for preschoolers. They'll get nightmares. I know. I have kids," Dennis reminded her. "Kids have to grow up before they're ready for reality."

"By then it's too late. Their beliefs have already been set by the trash they were fed in childhood. Look at teenage girls who grew up on fairy tales. They expect some man's gonna rescue them from whatever bad circumstances they come from, and they have no clue what *happily ever after* even looks like, because nobody writes kids' books about how marriages can actually turn out. Boredom, abuse, theft, in-laws, your spouse's friends constantly hanging around, coping with someone's addictions, being cheated on, forced into living beyond your means, going broke because of someone else's bills or overspending . . . Kids should be prepared for that shit. But parents aren't any help, the way they put on the big *everything's okay* act for their kids. Then when reality doesn't measure up after they leave, they either put on the same phony act as their parents, or get into drugs, drinking, and screwing around."

"That's pretty bleak. And you blame all of that on *Cinderella?*"

"Yeah. Though maybe no story prepares you for life. But it doesn't mean we shouldn't try showing it a little closer to what it could be. Which I've done." Marcie tossed him her version of *Tom the Tomcat* and her folder of drawings for *Conrad Crane.* "Just so you know, I sent these off to publishers."

"You can't—"

"Yours is *Tim*; mine's *Tom*. They're different."

Dennis leafed through the pages, shaking his head.

"We won't be competing," Marcie assured Dennis. "These are for more of a local market. They might not even get accepted."

"Do what you want. But you gotta redo my *Tim*."

"Fine. So you came all the way down here just to tell me that?"

"Email didn't seem to be working. And, no. Though I thought you might be a little happier to see me." Dennis stepped closer.

"I would have been. The timing was just bad."

"Evidently."

Her phone rang again. Dwayne!

"I got awesome news. I start next month in Orlando!" Dwayne announced.

"You're kidding!" Marcie watched Dennis stare up at the ceiling, likely able to tell the caller was yet another man. "That's awesome!"

"Hey, can you go there and find us a place?"

"Absolutely! In what price range? I don't want to spend much more than four-hundred for my half." Less than what she'd paid here, but if she could, she'd prefer to pay less. So she could save. Just in case.

"See what you can find for twelve or thirteen."

Cinderella lived after all. "Where's your new bank? So I can look near where you'll work and you won't have to commute."

"Anywhere around the lake'll be great."

"I'll pack up here and head out as soon as I can."

"Keep me posted."

"I will! I can't wait!"

"Me either!"

"Who was that?" Dennis asked, when she ended the call.

"A man I'll be living with in Orlando."

"Well. I won't keep you. Just remember what you said about *Cinderella*."

"I will."

"Does he carry a gun?"

"No, he's a banker."

"I hope he's better than the punk you have now." Dennis finished his beer, set the can down on the table, stood, and walked toward the door.

"Where're you going?"

"To a hotel."

"You don't have to."

"I'd feel safer. Plus, you have enough boyfriends. I don't want to get a disease."

"I'm sorry all this had to happen just when you came," Marcie apologized.

"I should have said I was coming."

And then Dennis walked out. Probably the last time she'd see him, but life moved on. She'd have Dwayne, and Dennis would still be a business partner. Marcie pedalled off to go rent a car.

"How was your day?" Pat asked, when he got home from the bank and found Marcie packing. Then he looked around. "Where's your bike?"

"In the car."

"What car?"

Marcie pointed to her rental in the parking lot. "I'm leaving tomorrow."

"You're gonna drive back to Canada?"

"No. Florida still. I just need a fresh start."

"Can't say I blame you. Where're you going?"

Marcie shrugged. "I dunno. Probably just drive around for a while and see where I end up." She didn't want him inadvertently tipping off Emilio, who could hunt her down or put the word out statewide to his gangster friends and have one of them show up at her new place and wreck everything with Dwayne.

"Oh." Pat looked devastated. "I'll miss you. Can I at least take you out for dinner first?"

"I need to pack and get to bed. I want an early start in the morning."

Like before Emilio came over.

In Orlando, Marcie bought a new phone and called Dwayne from it, because she didn't want any ghosts from her Tampa past phoning her either.

Dwayne didn't answer. Maybe because he didn't recognize the new number. "Hi, Dwayne. It's Marcie. I got a new phone. Call me back. I'm in Orlando! Just gonna start apartment hunting. This place is gorgeous!" And it was. Cycling paths all around the lake with people on them. Boats in the water. Paradise on a more monied level.

Marcie dragged her bike out of the back seat, along with her cash box, so no one would steal it out of the car, then rode around looking for For Rent signs. At the first place she saw, she rang the building manager's buzzer and asked, "How much are your two-bedrooms?" She'd need her own room to paint in.

The price fell within budget. "Can I see it?"

It was beautiful. More luxurious than anywhere she'd ever dreamed of living. New laminate floors, a brick wall in the living room, huge windows, views of both the lake and the courtyard with a swimming pool, square sinks in the shiny-tiled bathrooms, marble counters there and in the kitchen, and one of those stoves with the elements painted on. "This is perfect. We'll take it. I just have to phone my fiancé . . ."

Saying that sounded so strange and phony: a charade. But Dwayne and their life together was real. She had to act with her head more than with what the cells in her body—contaminated and programmed for cynicism through their lifetime of negative experience—were saying. That this was just another man-scam.

". . . so he can send you a cheque for his part of the rent and deposit. What's your address?"

Yet, the pit of intuitive gloom spread. That feeling she got when something wasn't going to work out. She just didn't know how her body knew it ahead of time, although it couldn't, really. There was no logical reason to think Dwayne wouldn't come through. He'd phoned while she'd still been in Tampa and told her to do this, and an hour during the day while Dwayne was at work wasn't such an unreasonable length of time for him not to respond to her call. Her intuition had to be wrong. Patterns *did* break. Look at Stan. He was awesome. Nice, attractive, real, and he'd followed through on what he said. Okay, he was married—that might make a difference—but maybe this was just what taking any risk felt like. Like bungee jumping: the perceptual system cried suicide, even though the brain knew the ankles were tied to a sturdy, secure rope.

But she didn't know Dwayne. Really. She hoped, believed, and gambled somewhat, but not enough to secure the apartment.

She called Dwayne again, yet he didn't answer this time either. The bank would now be closed in Chicago, but she was calling on his cell phone. Maybe he'd gone home and left it at work? When voice mail, once again, invited her to leave a message, Marcie, doing her best to keep her pessimism at bay, said, "I found us a gorgeous place. I have the address where you can send the cheque.

I'll pay the landlord my part when he gets yours and we can move in any time!"

And that was all she could do for now. The rest of the day, she rode around the lake, found a place for dinner, then a cheap hotel to sleep for the night, because there was no room to stretch out in her car. All the while, her phone remained silent. Maybe there was something wrong with it. Maybe it had stopped receiving incoming calls. She used the phone in her room to call herself. Her phone rang.

In the morning, she tried Dwayne again, when the bank would be open, so if he had left his phone there, he'd have it again. This time, instead of Dwayne's voice saying he wasn't able to take calls right now, a computer voice told her "The number you have dialled is no longer in service."

Marcie froze in shock, even though she'd been warned by that sense of foreboding. Could she have misdialled? She tried again, and got the same message. Then tried Dwayne on his office landline. Maybe he was having trouble with his service provider.

When would she ever stop making excuses for men?

A message informed her which branch she'd reached, and if she knew the extension of the person she was trying to reach, please enter it now. She did and subsequently heard, "Hi, you've reached Dwayne Richards. I've either stepped away from my desk for a moment or am on the other line. Please leave a message." He was likely screening his calls and ignoring anything from Florida. "Hi, Dwayne. It's Marcie. I'm in Orlando. Your cell's no longer in service. Call me."

There was one more thing to test. Then she'd give up. And probably never believe a promise an unmarried man made again. After breakfast, Marcie asked the desk clerk to borrow a phone book, paper, and pen. She looked up the name of Dwayne's bank and wrote down all the branch addresses and phone numbers in Orlando. When returning the directory, she asked, "Which ones are near here?" and was given a map. Marcie plotted the addresses, like she'd done with the bookstores and art galleries in Tampa, then biked to the closest branch. "Do you have a Dwayne Richards starting work here? He just transferred from Chicago?" The teller asked someone who asked someone else and eventually returned with an answer of no.

The same thing happened at every branch.

Marcie walked out of the last bank in total disbelief. What a *fucking ass*! Lying bastard! Why did men do that? The same thing had happened to her before. It was how she'd ended up living in Calgary. In the last fourteen years, she thought she might have become a little more adept at evaluating men. Dwayne had seemed different. Which obviously didn't mean better. Just a con in a different way. Did his twisted mind get off on imagining a woman acting on whatever he said? Or had a part of him really wanted to leave Chicago and live with her, but chickened out in the end? Maybe men had their weird fantasies, too. She just couldn't figure out what they were or how she incited them, or maybe she somehow asked for the treatment she kept getting over and over again. Or she just had bad taste in men. Something had gone wrong with her hardwiring, making her unattracted to reliable, stable guys who weren't afraid of making a commitment.

Or, maybe it all boiled down to status. Bankers didn't marry waitresses. Or artists. Or at least not until they were famous. At least she hadn't left much behind in Tampa. Hell, if she wanted, she could turn around and go back. To Emilio? A generous con artist who at least wanted her and kept showing up on a regular basis, though his *largesse* truly was a concern. To living next door to a man she yearned for but who hated her because of an accident of genetics? To sharing a crowded apartment with Pat? Yes, there were some stores she'd developed working relationships with, where she sold her artwork, but every city had gift shops, and Florida had tons of ports where cruise ships docked. She could just as easily sell art and milk the portrait cow elsewhere. Like on a beach. So, yes, she wanted to leave Tampa and start fresh elsewhere in Florida. Dwayne had just accelerated the gamble. But still, he'd acted incredibly shitty. Although, she supposed she had to thank him for a great cruise and a lot of portrait work. Had she really expected to live happily ever after with anyone? No. But for a while, she had hoped Dwayne might just be the one.

After recovering enough composure to speak without her voice cracking, she called Stan. "Hey, I'm in Orlando."

"Awesome! You're only three and a half hours away. You can be here by tonight." He gave her the address of his hotel in Fort Lauderdale.

"How was your trip?" He hugged her when she stepped into the lobby. He'd been working on his laptop there, waiting for her. His kindness made her cry all over again.

Up in their room, after sex, she spilled the whole story. "Why do men do that?"

"Because they can." Stan shrugged. He told her some of the cruel things women had done to him before he got married. "Some people are just assholes. You hungry?"

"Yeah. I haven't eaten since breakfast."

After breakfast the next morning, Stan asked if she wanted to go sit on the beach, which was right out back of the hotel!

"We're practically the only ones here," Marcie noted, when setting foot on the sand.

"Yeah, it's January. Seventy's too cold for most people."

Marcie watched the little waves lapping onto the beach, which stretched almost to the horizon, then bolted off across the sand to go play in them. "I've always wanted to do this!" she cried. Run forever on the surf line, just like in travel brochures. She tossed Stan her camera and kept going until the waves crashed into her knees. When they swelled to waist height, Marcie threw herself into them and let herself be sucked out to sea, then slammed back onto the sand with the next wave. She was awed at the power of the water. The next wave towered over her head. Gleeful, she let it crash onto her, the swam out over the next swells until she reached the last one in the sequence, which she rode in on. It picked up speed on its drive to the beach and smashed her into the shore even harder, leaving her breathless and hurting a little. She was falling in love with Florida all over again. The east coast was a way better place for her, and she had not just Stan, but Chrissy, to thank for that. Had the woman not suggested getting out of the car on the Veterans Expressway, she would never have met Stan.

The water died down again and she walked back to Stan. "I got some great shots of you." He tapped her camera. Mementos she could look back on and relive the body-surfing experience all over again.

She squeezed him in a sandy, wet hug. Only then did she recall the possible presence of sharks.

Back on their collapsible chairs, Stan did some work on his laptop, while Marcie sketched Tim the Tomcat riding the current of the Bow River through downtown Calgary on an upside-down cowboy hat, having a great time as people looked on and waved. Tim crashing a picnic in Stanley Park. Tim whooping it up at a Stampede breakfast. Tim looking a little nauseous on his free ride up the Calgary Tower. Tim riding in the rodeo snuggled up to a barrel rider. Marcie would add more wholesome adventures after lunch, then send him back happy to his happy home. Just like Dennis wanted. She photographed her sketches, then asked Stan if she could use his laptop to send Dennis an email.

Over lunch in the hotel dining room, they plotted their route to the Keys around tourist destinations they wanted to stop at. After lunch, Marcie drove to a storage depot, rented a locker, returned her rental car, and phoned Stan to come pick her up so they could head out.

At the end of their trip, Marcie said good-bye to Stan at the airport, after transferring his rental car to her name. "Thanks." She kissed him on the cheek. "For everything. I feel like I've learned lots from you and even become a new person."

"A pleasure. You're really fun. Stay in touch."

"You have my new number?" she confirmed.

Part of that "everything" Stan had done for her was to be a reference so she could rent a place. Plus, Palm Grove should put in a good word. But where did she want to settle? Nothing in her life was forever, so why not start where she was? Ft. Lauderdale was a big city, with a port, and lots of beaches. As—or if—things became untenable here, she could work her way south, community by beachside community. The possibilities should last her a lifetime.

About the Author

Marilynn spent her early years in Southern Ontario, where she left home young to make her way in Alberta, working in the hospitality industry and, after a brief stint in Florida, now resides in BC.

She did her first year of post-secondary at the University of Waterloo, where she swam varsity, and obtained her B.Ed. from the University of Calgary, where she also studied creative writing with Aritha van Herk and Fred Wah. To keep fit, she regularly weight trains and has dabbled in various other sports, like motorcycling, ping-pong, rowing, and skateboarding. As thrills of a lifetime, she has flown a fighter-jet trainer plane (with a pilot) and driven Lamborghini on a track. For thirty-three years she has kept a large parrot.

Marilynn has travelled a bit, but with scent and food sensitivities, she prefers staying home.

Art has been an ongoing passion for Marilynn. For ten years, she modelled for art classes and has a website on Art Artists Artwork. She displays and sometimes sells and rents work through local galleries. Currently, she earns her living as a tutor and sometimes barista.

Printed in Great Britain
by Amazon